Basic Instincts

NOW COMES THE DARK

THOM COLLINS

ENTWINED PUBLISHING

Now Comes the Dark
ISBN # 978-1-80250-723-2
©Copyright Thom Collins 2025
Cover Art by Kelly Martin ©Copyright February 2025
Interior text design by Entwined Publishing
Published by Evidence, an Entwined Publishing imprint

Published in 2025 by Entwined Publishing, United Kingdom.

Entwined Publishing is a division of Totally Entwined Group Limited.

NOW COMES THE DARK

Chapter One

The Viaduct

By eleven-thirty on Friday night, wallowing in the heat and scent of dozens of excited bodies and listening to the driving beat of one seamless dance track after another at a club called Sash, Roman realised he was horny. No big surprise. It was a near-permanent state for him most days, but tonight, the urge was stronger than ever. He wanted to feel skin against his skin, hot breath in his face, the hardness of one groin pressing into his.

He needed a man…and badly.

"I'm gonna move on," he told his flatmate, having to shout directly into Ashley's ear to be heard above the deafening music.

"We're about to order another round," Ashley yelled back, not taking his eyes off his boyfriend Patrick, who was deep in conversation with a muscle-man Roman didn't recognise.

"You stay. I'm fine on my own."

Ashley looked at him sideways, reluctant to take his attention off Patrick completely. "You know it's not safe out there. Stay here with us. There's another cabaret starting soon."

"I'll be fine. I'm not going far."

Now Ashley gave him his full interest. "You're not going to The Viaduct. Please tell me you're not."

Roman nodded. "I've had enough of it in here. It's too noisy. But you stay. Enjoy it."

"That place is a sewer," Ashley grimaced. "A shithole. Only freaks and sluts go in there."

Roman patted his friend on the shoulder. "That's what I'm hoping for. Have a good night. I'll see you in the morning, if not before."

"If you're still in one piece," Ashley retorted before giving a reluctant nod. "Be careful...in every way."

With a smile of reassurance, Roman slipped away.

As always, Sash was packed. It was Roman's least favourite venue in the city, and he had to edge and slither his way through the crowd to reach the door. There was a queue six deep at the bar, while a DJ in full club-kid drag ignored the punters and focused on the music with life-or-death gravity. Roman didn't care for this place at the best of times. The drinks were overpriced, and the atmosphere was more than a little crazed. Tomorrow would be the first Saturday in weeks when he didn't have to go to work. A rare opportunity. He could stay out late, until the early hours, and didn't want to waste his time in here, especially when his dick was calling the shots.

There was zero chance of him hooking up in Sash. The cliental were too self-important, too bloody cool or out of their minds on drugs to indulge in face-to-face flirting. They came in their packs and cliques and never broke rank. The only way to get off with someone else in the bar was through an app, and even then, the chances were slim.

He made it to the door and burst into the street, relieved as it swung shut behind him, deadening the relentless soundtrack. The cold of late October was a relief after the extreme heat of the bar. He inhaled, drawing cool air deep into his lungs. He would have left much earlier if he'd had the chance. When Ashley had realised Roman was coming out tonight, he'd insisted on dragging him along with his awful boyfriend and their cackling friends, no matter how much he'd objected.

At last, he was free to enjoy the kind of night he wanted.

Despite the time — getting on for midnight — the traffic was heavy in both directions. Roman made it to the centre of the road and waited his chance to cross to the other side. There were plenty of people on the streets, though most of them moved around in groups between one venue and another. The gay village of Blyham was no longer considered to be the safe LGBTQ space it used to be, but Roman had no fear of walking around on his own, not when there were so many others about. He stuck to the main streets and knew where to avoid.

The Viaduct was located on the opposite side, down the steeply sloping street, at the intersection of Salvin Road and Broad Street. When he arrived, there were six men waiting to get in, and he joined the line behind them. It was a slow wait. The Viaduct was for members only, and it always caused a delay when a new member tried to sign up at the door.

Roman shivered and hugged himself. The cold air had caused his nipples to harden and peak the front of his pale blue T-shirt. At least that would be good for some attention once he got inside. He cast his eyes over the men in front of him. There were a mixed bunch of ages and sizes. None of them caught his immediate interest.

Roman wasn't sure what kind of man he was in the mood for tonight, but he would know him when he saw him. There was a time when he would have settled for any guy who paid him attention, regardless of age or body type. As long as they weren't totally ugly, he used to oblige. Roman had been younger then — and a lot skinnier.

At six feet tall, with a naturally slim build and large nose, he'd spent most of his teens and early twenties feeling awkward and unworthy. That had all changed a couple of years ago. When he was twenty-four, his body unexpectedly filled out, and his face, previously drawn and uninteresting, matured into something more traditionally handsome. Though he had never been an ugly duckling, he suddenly transformed into a hunk. Almost overnight he got attention from the kind of men who wouldn't have looked at him before.

Roman didn't have a preference or type. He wasn't hung up on looks, physique or huge dicks, but he had reached a stage where he could become more discerning about the men he fucked. He could take his pick and no longer had to settle for whatever was on offer. It was a liberating change of circumstance. He didn't think he was vain, but being considered hot brought a lot of advantages he didn't have before. It was like a new-found super-power, and he had revelled in it. He still did and wasn't ready to settle tonight.

He was horny as hell and wanted a man who would satisfy his every primal, base need.

By the time he reached the front of the line, his skin was rippled with gooseflesh, and he stepped into the foyer, grateful for the warmth. He showed his membership card to the attendant on the door and paid the entry fee. Fridays and Saturdays were the most expensive days of the week. Roman had a feeling, though, that tonight would be worth it.

The Viaduct was located in the lower vaulted cellars of Old Elvet Bridge, a railway bridge that ran through the centre of the city. The street-level entrance opened onto a small, low-ceilinged cloakroom and changing area. Throughout the week, the club ran a variety of theme nights, ranging from leather to sportswear and jock straps. Members had the option of going fully naked at any time. Fridays were more relaxed and mainstream. The dress code was topless. The men who arrived before him had stripped down to underwear and sneakers. Two of them wore backless briefs, displaying their wide, juicy arses.

Dispensing with the changing room, Roman pulled his T-shirt over his head and stuffed it into his waistband, bait enough to attract what he was looking for. If not, he would strip down to his underpants later.

The Viaduct had a smell like nowhere else in Blyham. The stone vaults had a permanent odour of damp, combined with the aroma of stale booze, sweat, poppers and aftershave. It was an intense aphrodisiac. He breathed it in, and his cock stiffened with anticipation of what might come. With a quickening pulse, he passed through the dark, beaded curtain to the next room.

The bar area and small dancefloor were busy but nowhere near as packed as Sash had been. He found it easy to move through the crowd and make an order. Unlike other places, the bar was not where the real action took place. Porn scenes played on large monitors around the room, but Roman had little interest in watching them. He'd come for more active involvement.

As he waited for his beer, he cast his eyes around the dimly lit interior, searching for a potential fuck-buddy. Several sets of interested eyes stared back at him. A couple of guys in the corner had potential. They leaned against a beer barrel and looked him up and down. *Not bad.* They were in their early thirties, gym-built but not too big. He couldn't decide if they were together. Couples could be fun when everyone involved had the right attitude and knew what they were getting into, but in his experience, it was rarely worth the effort. It could also get extremely messy, especially if he was into one half of the partnership more than the other.

Physically, this pair were well matched, but it was too early for him to make a decision.

He wouldn't settle until he found out who else was available.

Of the dozen or so men gathered in the bar, there was no one who piqued his interest.

Roman finished his beer and began his search.

On the far side of the room, a door led outside to a small yard — the smoking area. He walked straight by and took the narrow, stone staircase up to the first floor. This level occupied a larger section of vaults than the room below and was a network of low ceilings and archways. He'd heard in the past, centuries ago, that the vaults beneath the bridge had stored grain and silk. It had been a refuge for the homeless and destitute and at one time had served as the cells of the first Blyham prison.

Now it was an illicit labyrinth of sex.

In the largest room, illuminated by red lights and more screens showing a variety of different porn films, was the main play area. A middle-aged man lay in a sling, his legs hoisted high and wide. He was naked except for boots, a black jockstrap and a blindfold. A skinny guy with his jeans around his ankles fucked him while a group stood around to watch or wait their turn.

In the opposite corner, a young man lay in a copper bathtub while two guys pissed all over him. An older man was bent over the spanking bench, groaning in pleasure each time his ample arse was struck from behind.

This level of kink was not for Roman...not tonight. He wanted straightforward man-on-man action. He wanted to get fucked and not for the amusement of all these hungry eyes.

He wandered deeper into the complex. Guys loitered in the archways, squeezing their crotches, enticing him into the smaller chambers behind with their curtains and vinyl-covered beds. No one spoke. The only exchanges were physical—a look, a touch, a suggestive gesture.

In the dim light, he recognised a guy he'd hooked up with a few weeks back—handsome, dark hair. *John or Jack or something like that.* Not that names mattered much. Roman took it as a given that most of the men he had sex with pretended to be someone they were not. It worked both ways, and he rarely revealed much about himself, either. No one came to The Viaduct for friendship or a companion. What he remembered most about John or Jack was that he'd claimed to be a top with a nine-inch cock who would fuck Roman like he'd never been fucked in his life. The size of his cock was no exaggeration, but when they had got back to Roman's room, he had flopped onto his back, pulled his knees into his chest and begged Roman to destroy his hole. Roman had obliged to save the hook-up from being a total waste of time, but he would not be fooled twice. He knew what he wanted tonight, and a well-hung bottom was not on his wish list.

With a nod of acknowledgement, he moved on.

None of the men he found in the tunnels were right—too young, too old, too butch, too many tattoos, too many piercings. Some were too bald, and others wore their hair too long. On any other night he would have slipped into one of the private vaults without a thought, guided only by his dick. But tonight, it was no good. He wasn't just looking for sex. He could get that any time. He wanted a man to excite him, someone irresistible, a man he would beg for.

None of these fit the bill.

The upper level of The Viaduct was identical to this floor with one exception. It was pitch black. There was no point in him going up there. He needed to be able to see the man he wanted.

Undeterred, he returned to the bar. The night was early. The Viaduct wouldn't close until four. He could wait.

The lower floor was fuller than before, and at least down here, guys were prepared to talk to one another. The couple who had spied him earlier, gave him the eye all over again. They put their heads together and whispered as they watched him, staring with intent. Roman ignored them. He went back to the bar and ordered another beer before securing a spot in the corner from where he could see the comings and goings of the front door, the smoking yard and the staircase.

He didn't know why he was so restless tonight. He usually came here with a single purpose—to get in, hook up, unload and get out. There were dozens of attractive, fuckable guys around, and he could have had a good time with any of them. But none of them were *the one*. It was like a shopping trip, when he didn't really know what he wanted but would know it when he saw it.

Five minutes later, he did.

The man who stepped through the curtain at the entrance was not the most perfect, but the sight of him sent a bolt of raw energy all through Roman. It coiled like a snake around his stomach and groin. *God damn.*

That's him. He's the one.

The guy was in his mid-to-late thirties. His square jaw and cleft chin were coated in dark stubble. His thick, dark hair was dishevelled. This was not the kind of bloke who spent hours in front of the mirror making sure every hair was in place before going out. His torso was bare. A white shirt hung from the waistband of his jeans, dangling from the right hip. He had a naturally strong build with muscular shoulders and a good chest, his stomach was flat, but there was no six-pack. He didn't need to spend hours in the gym to pump and grind his confidence. It exuded from him in waves.

Roman guzzled his beer, unable to take his eyes off the stranger.

He's the sexiest fucking thing I've seen...ever.

He watched as the man cast his eyes in a lazy sweep around the bar, beginning at the other side.

Roman straightened, tightened his abs and stuck out his chest. He raised his chin and turned his head, waiting for the man's gaze to come in his direction.

In the last two years, Roman was used to having men fall at his feet, and he'd pick anyone he desired. It had become too easy. As he waited for the stranger to look his way, he was no longer a hot, self-assured twenty-six-year-old, but the skinny dweeb of five years earlier, the one who had struggled to find his place. His confidence deserted him.

At last, the man looked at him, and his eyes lingered. There was an intense, humourless quality to his face. Sexy as fuck, but kind of scary, too. Outside of The Viaduct, Roman would have been wary, unsure whether this guy was going to fuck him to death or punch him unconscious.

Roman was frozen in the force of his stare.

The man's mouth twitched at the corner before it turned into a devasting smirk.

Then he walked away, giving the room one last look-over before heading to the stairs and the upper levels.

Before he knew what he was doing, Roman was halfway across the floor in pursuit.

Chapter Two

"Get home safely."

When Roman reached the bottom of the stairs, the man had already disappeared around the upper bend. He raced up the steps to the first floor. The playroom was much busier than before. Where had all these men come from? His eyes searched for the stranger, but he was impossible to find among the mass of near-naked torsos. Guys huddled together, kissing, groping, playing with each other's dicks. There were men on their knees sucking or being jizzed on.

The stranger couldn't have succumbed to the action already. He had only been out of sight for ten, maybe fifteen seconds.

Roman pushed forward, turning his head in every direction. His insides tightened as his urgency increased.

"Hey, sexy," a man whispered in his ear. He slid a rough hand around Roman's waist and spun him around so they faced each other. Now both hands were on Roman's arse, pulling their hips together. The man ground his hard bulge against Roman's groin.

It was no good. This guy was in his late forties, a skin-headed man-mountain of steroid-boosted muscle. Even if Roman hadn't already set his sights on one particular man, he wouldn't have been interested in this fella.

"Sorry," he said, putting a hand on the man's enormous chest to push him away. It was like being trapped in King Kong's grip.

"Don't be like that, boy," the man said, coming in for a kiss. His breath was dire — garlic, alcohol and bacterial infection. "I've got something that will rearrange your insides."

"No," he yelled forcefully, causing those nearest them to turn and look. The man let go and raised his hands, grinning, like it was all a cheeky game.

"Calm down." His tone was condescending. "I'm just fucking with you. Shit, you pretty boys are all the same."

Roman could have said something similar about roid-heads but held his tongue. The prick wasn't worth the effort, and every second wasted could cost him the prize.

He pressed onwards, covering the room as fast as possible. The same man as before was in the sling, getting it from a guy Roman had previously hooked up with. A bigger queue had now formed to take a turn on the open arse, and a large crowd had gathered to watch the spectacle. The man in the sling seemed to love every second, begging to be fucked harder. *That arse must be very loose by now.*

He scanned the faces of the crowd around the sling. His stranger wasn't among them.

He didn't find him at the spanking bench or the piss trough. Roman cast a final glance around the room, making certain he was not there, before pressing into the deeper vaults. He hoped he hadn't gone upstairs to the dark zone. If he had, there was no hope of finding him.

He wondered why he was so intent on catching this guy, when he'd seen him for less than a minute, and they'd only exchanged eye contact for a few seconds? *Because seconds is all it takes.* There had been an instant spark…chemistry. They would be dynamite together. The man would be a great fuck. He knew that instinctively. Roman wasn't interested a quick suck or a lacklustre fumble in the dark. He wanted to fuck, to make a real connection for however short a time. This man was it. He'd seen it his eyes and in that arrogant smirk. The two of them were destined to get together. It was fate.

And the chase was exhilarating. Roman was so used to men coming after him that it was an unexpected thrill to reverse their roles.

I'll find you, Mister. And when I do, we'll both be grateful for it.

The tunnels were busier now, with men lining the walls on either side, leaning, watching, presenting themselves. Roman checked their faces keenly. There were some he recognised and many he didn't. Some men mistook the cause of his interest and stepped towards him, ready to accept the unspoken invitation. He shook his head and continued.

Some of the arches had their curtains closed. Did he dare pull them aside to see who was behind? It was an established rule of the club that such behaviour was a no-no. The curtains were closed for a reason, privacy. He had to accept that, however just his action might be.

No, he warned himself. *Be respectful.*

Roman's pulse quickened with every step. He had almost reached the end. Only a few more arches then the stairs up to the dark zone. He was running out of options.

A bunch had gathered outside the last vault in the tunnel. He knew what that meant. Whoever was inside hadn't closed the curtain and was putting on a show. He studied the faces of the voyeurs and recognised a couple, but not the one he wanted. Roman inched closer, stretching to get a look inside.

The room had the same dimensions as the rest, small with the stone, arched ceiling and floor, a vinyl-covered bench at the back. The man — Roman's man — sat on the bench. His head rested against the wall. His jeans were around his ankles, his thighs and knees spread wide. He was sexier than Roman had first appreciated. His eyes were half closed, and his mouth was open in a down-turned kind of smile that created sharp, little dimples in his cheeks.

But there was somebody with him.

Roman's soul deflated. He was too late.

Motherfucker.

Someone knelt on the floor in front of him, dressed in nothing but a white jockstrap and sneakers. His dark head was buried in the stranger's crotch, moving back and forth in a dipping motion. His face was obscured, but Roman knew exactly who had stolen his prize. His creamy, round arse was unmistakable with his tattoos, FUCK on the left cheek and ME on the right. Cameron Taylor.

The little slut.

He might have known that, of all the guys here, Cameron would have homed in on the man he wanted.

The stranger put one hand on the back of Cameron's head, guiding the pace and motion, looking down at him with half-closed eyes. Roman rose onto his toes, hoping for a better angle, wanting to see the man's cock, but Cameron's head blocked the view. Cameron was in his element, not just performing a blow job for the recipient but putting on a show for the spectators. He arched his back and raised his arse, widening his knees enough to open his buttocks and expose his hole.

Jealousy sickened Roman to the pit of his stomach.

He had never hooked up with Cameron. Despite being a similar age and Cameron's incredible good looks, Roman had never found him attractive. They were too alike in many ways — the hottest, freshest boys on the scene, the ones everyone else desired.

Roman couldn't watch anymore. He couldn't bear to see his closest rival enjoy the thing he craved the most.

Cameron might as well have poured a bucket of iced water on Roman's dick.

He pushed his way back down the tunnel. It was time to leave.

* * * *

Roman sat in the beer garden of a pub called Julie's and nursed a double vodka and Coke. He was alone. He had no enthusiasm to return to Sash and catch up with his friends, but it was his first weekend off in months, and he wasn't ready to go home, either. Julie's was friendly and unpretentious. They played chart music and camp classics, and the bar appealed to lesbians and indie kids — a world away from the preening posers in Sash.

He checked the dating apps on his phone with little gusto. He had wanted to make a true connection with a real person tonight, not swipe on some rando he could meet any day of the week. With a sigh, he shoved the phone in his pocket.

It was quarter to two. The pub was winding down to closing. There were about fifteen other people scattered around the beer garden in groups, laughing and having fun. Music poured through the open door from the main bar, where a drag DJ was taking her final requests of the night. Roman wondered whether to get a last drink here before final orders, or to move on to The New Inn, which stayed open until three at the weekend.

"What's the matter with your face?" the manager, Phil, asked as he came around collecting empty glasses.

His voice broke the self-pitying spell Roman had fallen under, and he raised a smile. "Ah, you know what's it like. It's been a long night."

"We don't usually see you in here on Fridays." Phil put his glasses down on Roman's table and sat beside him.

"Weekend off."

"I wish I knew what one of those was. All right for some, eh?" Phil was almost forty with a neat beard that was running to salt and pepper and a slender build. He was very good-looking and lots of Roman's friends fancied him, but Roman saw him more as a caring uncle than a fuck-buddy. He would hate to ruin their friendship with an impulsive hook-up. "So why exactly is your face like a smacked arse?"

Roman laughed. Like all great bartenders, Phil had the knack of reading people like books. "I've just come from The Viaduct."

Phil grimaced. "Now it makes sense. I'd be miserable too if I'd been in that shithole."

"It's not that bad."

"It's not good. Why does a boy like you want to waste his time in a dump like that? You know you can take your pick from the best guys in the village."

"Because I'm not always a nice boy," Roman said. "Not all the time, anyway." *Tonight, I wanted to make a real pig of myself. It just wasn't meant to be.*

"You can still do better than going there," Phil warned, giving his arm a reassuring pat. "So, what else have you got planned for your exciting weekend of freedom?"

"Not a lot. A long lie-in tomorrow. Catch up on TV and probably come out again tomorrow night."

"You're on your own now? You're not planning to walk home by yourself, are you?"

Roman shrugged. "Probably, yeah…if it stays dry."

"Don't. Get a taxi. Didn't you hear? Another lad had the shit kicked out of him last weekend. The fuckers broke his nose and knocked out a couple of teeth."

"Shit. No, I hadn't heard. Did you know him?"

"He comes in here sometimes, though I doubt he will again. If it were me, I'd stay far away from here. You know that's the fourth attack in the village in the last three months alone. And it's only four months since Charles Lear was murdered. I swear this place is going to hell."

Roman nodded, lost for anything to say. In the last year and a half, an atmosphere of fear and dread had developed in the Blyham LGBTQ community with an increase in homophobic hate crime. The horror had increased over the summer when the police publicly linked the recent murder of Charles Lear to the unsolved deaths of four other local men over an eighteen-month period. The gay men of Blyham weren't just being beaten up for their sexuality. They were being killed for it.

"Did they catch anyone?" he asked at last. "For the assault last weekend?"

"The police in this city? You're joking, aren't you? They haven't even sent an officer around to the bars to ask for witnesses or CCTV. They don't give a shit what happens to us. We need to take care of ourselves, which is why you're getting a taxi home tonight, okay?"

Roman nodded. "Sure. Of course I will. Where did it happen? Last weekend?"

"Somewhere around Rupert Street. The lad was heading home to the East End when a bunch of arseholes jumped him. They didn't even take his wallet, from what I've heard. They were only interested in beating him up. And it's not just boys walking home alone that are at risk. Last month, a couple of visitors heading back to their hotel were attacked. Don't go thinking there's safety in numbers. You need a car to take you home, door to door."

"I'm listening. Don't worry."

Phil nodded and got to his feet, gathering up the empty glasses. "I hope you are. You've got far too handsome a face to have it rearranged by a gang of thugs. Look after yourself. I'll see you tomorrow night. Get home safely."

"Yeah, I will. Good night."

The evening had been a downer already. Roman's conversation with Phil had hammered a nail into its coffin. There was no point hanging around any longer. The New Inn and The Viaduct would close in another hour, and he didn't fancy going to Equator, the nightclub that stayed open until six. He might as well go home and hope for better luck tomorrow. Maybe the sexy guy from The Viaduct would make another appearance, and he'd have more success a second time. So what if he'd be picking up Cameron Taylor's cast-offs. Roman would prove to that man what a superior cock sucker he was compared to Cameron.

With an indignant smile, he finished his drink.

The drag queen turned off the music and the place quickly emptied. As he stood, he spotted a familiar face pass through the bar towards the exit. Will, another of his conquests from a few weeks back, looking pretty fine in a tight black shirt.

Will was in his early thirties and in the transitional period from cute boy next door to fuckable Daddy. Blond and square-jawed, with a rugby player physique, Will was one of his more memorable one-night stands. Roman remembered rimming that big beefy arse for ages before Will turned around and fucked him. Will was one of those hot tops who love to get their arse eaten.

Roman's appetite returned in a rush.

Will had appeared to be alone when he'd walked through the bar just now. Maybe tonight didn't have to be a dead loss. He'd been hoping for fresh meat, but he could do a lot worse than reconnect with Will. The thought of burying his face between those big butt cheeks until dawn got his cock raging.

Roman hurried through the empty bar and out through the front door.

The crowd had cleared from the street in front, already making their way towards the remaining open venues. He looked around in all directions, searching for that broad back in the black shirt, with the short blond hair. Will was nowhere in sight.

"Fuck." What was it with his luck tonight? He took his eye off a hot man for a few seconds, and he disappeared.

He didn't bother to check his phone. He and Will had not exchanged numbers, so there was no point trying to track him down that way. Just like the guy in The Viaduct, the chance to hook up with Will had gone.

There was nothing else for it. He would go home, have a wank and try to get a decent night's sleep.

Bearing in mind what Phil had just told him, he wouldn't take the risk of walking. The nearest taxi rank was at the far end of Salvin Road. He crossed the street and headed in that direction, hoping he could pick up a ride there. If not, the late bus at two-thirty would take him closer to home.

The night had grown colder, and he had no desire to walk all that way without a jacket, anyway. He breathed in the crisp air and thought about the two men who had gotten away.

Roman didn't notice the car that crawled along the kerb behind him, until it drew level. The windows were down. Two men leaned out of the passenger side, drunken leers plastered across their faces.

"Hey, pretty boy, how's it going?" one of the men called, making a kiss-kiss sound.

Overexcited laughter peeled from the inside.

Roman faced forward and kept walking. There was no one ahead of him. He was alone. Could this night get any worse?

"Hey. Hey, you. Are you deaf or something? We're trying to talk to you. How about being nice, faggot."

Shit.

Now he was in trouble.

Chapter Three

The Stranger

Roman kept walking. It was naïve, and he didn't have a hope in hell of making it to the safety of another bar or the taxi rank. Bloody stupid of him. He should have arranged for an Uber to take him home while he was still in the bar. Hadn't Phil warned him just minutes ago to take a car from door to door? He kept his head down and increased his pace, hoping the men would get bored and move on.

The car drew ahead of him before pulling onto the kerb. Two men jumped straight out, followed moments later by the driver.

Roman's pulse raced. He looked for an escape route, a place to run for, but the men formed a semicircle around him, forcing his back to the wall. They were an intimating bunch. The one who had called him a faggot was the largest of the three, a real no-neck meathead. He was white with a grubby-looking suntan and tattoos that covered his skin from the neck to his fingertips. The second was a gingery blond and bearded. Roman might have fancied him if he wasn't some scumbag about to kick his head in. The third guy was the ugliest of the three — short and puggy with a piggy nose and mean little eyes.

"What's your hurry?" the big man asked, shoving Roman in the shoulder. "Have you got something better to do than talk to us?"

Roman was seething inside. They were the kind of bullies found in any school yard — a few years older but just as stupid, the mean-spirited good-for-nothing jock types who love nothing better than picking on the weaker kids. His teenage years had been blighted by boys exactly like these. The faces might be different, but their toxic masculinity was painfully familiar.

"I don't want any trouble," Roman said, hating the feeble sound of his own voice. "I'm on my way home. Just let me past."

The short guy giggled while the other two puffed themselves up with bravado.

Arseholes. Three against one. Is that what it took to make these bastards feel like men?

Despite the dangers in Blyham, five murders in the last year and dozens of homophobic assaults, Roman hadn't considered himself to be at risk. It was something that happened to other people. He flitted about the village having fun, paying little attention to the warnings issued by Phil and the other old-timers. He had never once found himself in a sticky situation.

Until now.

And that was all it took. One mistake. These guys could kick the shit out of him and leave him for dead. There was nothing he could do to defend himself.

Surprise was all he had. Roman spun around and shot through the gap between the ginger guy and the short one. If he could make it back to Julie's, the bar might not have locked the door yet, and he would find sanctuary inside.

The men were quicker. One of them swept Roman's legs from under him with a deft kick, and he sprawled forward, breaking his fall and saving his face, while skinning his palms.

The men roared with delight.

"He's a feisty little cunt," one of them said.

Another grabbed the back of Roman's T-shirt and hauled him to his feet. Before Roman could resist, the short guy delivered a sharp fist to his guts. Roman doubled over, winded by the force of the punch. Bile surged at the back of his throat.

Shit. This is really happening. Even now, reeling from the first strike, he felt like an observer, as though watching himself from above...except he wasn't. He was slap bang in the middle of this cluster-fuck, and from the sound of their merriment, these bastards had barely gotten started.

"How many dicks have you munched on tonight?" the tall one asked, twisting Roman's T-shirt tighter. "Is that what you've been up, eh? Suckin' cocks? I bet it wasn't enough, not for a cocksucker like you."

"No chance," Ginger chipped in. "He can't get enough of it. I bet he's gagging for a dick now. No such thing as too much for these gay boys."

"How would you know?" Roman growled, unable to stop himself. Righteous anger possessed him. "Unless you're talking from experience. You look the type."

His insolence earned him another punch in the guts. Roman was ready for it this time and tensed his abs, easing the force behind the blow.

The tall man who held him by the scruff of his shirt delivered another fist to his back, just below the ribcage. Roman bellowed and dizziness overwhelmed him. *Now, I've had it.*

His vision returned in time to see an object fly through the air. He had barely grasped what it was when the bottle struck the ginger man on the back of the head. It hit his skull with a satisfying clunk. The man wavered then dropped to his knees, clutching his head.

"What the *fuck?*" the ginger man yelled.

A figure rushed out of the night and spun the shortest and ugliest of his tormentors around. Roman registered a crack of fist against skin and a sickening crunch before the man staggered backwards, covering his face with his hands. Blood gushed between the bastard's fingers.

"My nose," he screamed. "My nose, it's broken."

The grip on Roman's T-shirt loosened, and he pulled away from the tall man.

What the hell is happening?

It took his muddled brain seconds to get a handle on it. The guy from the club, the object of his desire, had appeared from nowhere. He'd already dealt with two of the aggressors. The big man made a swing for the stranger with his massive fist. His saviour ducked and sidestepped the blow before delivering an incredible kick to the man's groin. Despite what they had done to him, even Roman winced at the viciousness and force behind the kick.

A high-pitched scream cut through the night. All three men were out of it, one clutching his head, the other a broken nose and the third cupping his balls as tears streaked down his face.

"Get the fuck out of here," the stranger growled at them. He had an accent that Roman couldn't place.

Now was not the time to figure it out. "I've already called the police. They'll be here in minutes."

"You assaulted us," the ginger man wailed, getting unsteadily to his feet.

"And when the cops arrive, I'll tell them why," the man answered. "Self-defence. I recorded what you were up to on my phone before wading in. A homophobic attack will look great on your police record, don't you think? You can try to explain your side when you go in front of the magistrates' court. But it won't be as fun as when I talk to the papers and tell them how easily I kicked your asses."

The big guy straightened up. His breath was fast and irregular, but he appeared to be making a recovery. Without the element of surprise, Roman wondered how well the stranger would fare against them, however magnificent he'd already proved himself to be. The man was weighing up his options.

"Come on, big boy," the stranger said, adopting an assertive fighting stance. "Let's see what you've got?"

"I need a hospital," the little runt wailed. "I'm not kidding. My nose is broken."

The other two exchanged glances, as though working out whether they could take him together. The ginger one still had a hand on the back of his head.

The big man was the first to speak. "Screw this. Get in the car. It's not worth the fucking aggro."

His companions were quick to obey. They were out of their depths, and they knew it. The big man moved to the driver's side. "There'll be other nights, faggots. You won't be so lucky next time." He spat on the ground before getting behind the wheel.

Roman stared at the man who had saved him as they drove away. He tried to speak, but there were no words. His throat was paralysed.

"Come on," the stranger said, "before their egos get the better of them and they circle around for another shot."

"The police," Roman gasped at last. "You called the police."

"No. I didn't have time. And it turns out, I didn't need them." He took a gentle grip of Roman's arm and led him back down the road. "Come on. The New Inn will still be open. We need to get off the streets for now."

The man walked fast. Roman had trouble keeping up with him and couldn't stop from looking over his shoulder to see if his attackers were following. The road was clear.

"Thank you," he said at last. Now that the shock of the ordeal was sinking in, he felt a growing weakness all through his body. *I could have died there.* At best he'd have faced a trip to the hospital to fix several broken bones. Those men had been serious, and though he hadn't paid attention to all the hate crimes that had occurred in Blyham, he knew how badly beaten the survivors had been. And five men hadn't been lucky at all.

"Mallon," the man said. "My name is Mallon. I couldn't stand by and watch them get away with that."

"Thank you," he repeated. "I'm Roman. How...how did you do that? There were three of them. That could easily have ended differently."

"Boxing. Boot camps. I've been a fighter since I was a boy."

The New Inn was fifty yards ahead. Roman saw a group of customers outside, and relief rushed through him. People. His kind of people. They were safe — for now, at least.

He glanced at Mallon as they walked. His gaze was fixed in front. *A man with purpose and determination.* His expression was deadly serious, his jaw taut.

The New Inn was the most traditional of the bars in the village, with old wooden floors and dark wood panelling. The long, original bar led through to a more recent extension and conservatory with a beer garden. The DJ played a selection of songs from the 1970s and '80s, while the clientele of older gays stood around chatting. The bar area was packed. Mallon guided Roman through the crowd to the near-empty beer garden. Efficient heaters kept the night chill at bay.

"Stay here," Mallon said, releasing his arm once Roman was seated. "What do you want to drink?"

"Vodka. Diet Coke."

Mallon nodded and left him.

Roman wrapped his arms around himself and shivered, despite the warmth. *Fuck.* He'd never experienced anything as frightening in his entire life. Like any gay man, he was used to homophobia, but the abuse he'd experienced in the past had always been verbal — name calling and hateful comments. This was the first time he'd been threatened with physical danger. *And if Mallon hadn't turned up when he did?* Roman shuddered and his heart raced again.

His hands throbbed. Some of the skin was broken on both palms from when he'd fallen forward. He inspected the damage. It could have been a lot worse. He'd have to clean them up to avoid getting an infection.

Mallon returned a few minutes later and set a drink in front of Roman. "I got you a double. You'll need it."

"Thanks."

Mallon had a whisky for himself. He pulled out a chair and sat beside him. "Okay now?"

Roman looked at him properly for the first time. When he'd caught sight of him in The Viaduct, in the dim light and from across the room, he had fancied him straight away. That first impression didn't do justice to how hot he was up close. Roman was in shock and reeling from his ordeal, and he still fancied the hell out of him. Intense grey eyes gazed from beneath a slightly hooded brow, giving his handsome face an air of mystery and danger.

"I think so," Roman said, snapping back into focus. "Still shaken, I guess. I'll get over it." He sipped his drink. The vodka was cheap and harsh with a syrupy sweet mixer. It burned the back of his mouth and throat, but he swallowed it gratefully. Mallon was right, he did need it, more than he realised. He took a deeper drink.

Mallon sipped his whisky. Roman caught the slight grimace as he swallowed. He pulled out a packet of cigarettes and lit one. Roman didn't know many people who still smoked. It was so outdated and would usually put him off, but it would take more than that to turn him off Mallon.

He released a sigh. "I can't believe how lucky I am that you came along when you did."

Mallon nodded, his mouth set in a firm, serious line. "I was looking for you. I searched every room of The Viaduct for you, from the top to the bottom, even in the dark."

Roman coughed. "You did?"

Mallon nodded, exhaling smoke. "I had given up. Figured you'd found someone you liked more. I was on my way here for a nightcap when I saw the disturbance up the street. I didn't know it was you until I'd cracked that asshole's nose."

Despite the tension of the last half hour, Roman laughed. "You were looking for me? I was searching for you. I gave up when I found you in one of the vaults with Cameron. I figured you had found what you were looking for."

"Cameron?"

"Dark hair. Around my age. Mixed heritage. 'Fuck me' tattoo on his arse. He sucked your dick."

"Oh." A flicker of a smile. The suggestion of dimples in his cheeks. "He was just a...snack. Not even that. Terrible blow job. All teeth. I didn't even come."

Things had taken a surreal turn. Roman had gone from the shock of an assault to sporting an erection and feeling horny in a few short seconds. "I suppose I should be grateful. If it wasn't for your disappointment in Cameron, you might not have come looking for me."

"That's one way to look at it. Another way is...if I had found you, I would still be in the vaults fucking you, and you would never have encountered those assholes at all."

Roman blushed, uncomfortable with the rapid gear change. As attractive as he found Mallon, he was too shaken to think about sex. "I can't believe that happened to me. In all the time I've lived here, that's a first."

Mallon put an elbow on the table and rested his chin in his hand. "I've heard this a problem in your city. The violence. Yes?"

"It didn't used to be. I've been here for six years, first at university then for work. It was always a safe, tolerant city. It's only in the last eighteen months that things have taken a turn for the worst. I take it you are passing through. You don't live here?"

"I'm here for work. I don't know how long for. Just a week this time, but it may be longer in the future."

"Then it hasn't been a great introduction. Like I said, Blyham hasn't always been like this, but now... I don't know what to think. It's sad."

"Sad, yes. But no different to many other places." Mallon stubbed out the cigarette. "I travel a lot, and this kind of trouble is on the rise everywhere I go. As more far-right assholes come to power and run the countries, it gives the narrow-minded bigots, the intolerant minority, a sense of entitlement. They think they can do what they want. And most of the time they do, because they get away with it. You should learn to fight. Learn how to defend yourself. You might have to on another night."

Roman looked into those serious grey eyes. He didn't follow politics or have an allegiance to one party, but what Mallon said sounded true enough. The entire country seemed to teeter on the edge of a shit-pit of hate and violence. He doubted Blyham was worse than any other city. It was an all-pervasive problem.

Roman finished his drink in another mouthful. The taste was horrific, but the alcohol had a soothing effect on his nerves. Under different circumstances he would have been shy and uncomfortable sitting with a man he desired so much. Of the guys he had fucked in the last year, he struggled to remember a meaningful conversation. In an era of apps and hook-ups, talking to a stranger was rare.

As Mallon had saved his life, he figured they were beyond those awkward, getting-to-know-you moments.

He raised the empty glass. "Another? I'll get them this time."

Mallon gave a terse shake of his hand. His mouth turned downwards. "I'd rather not."

Disappointment struck like a slap in the face. "Oh."

Mallon banged his half-touched drink on the table. "This is piss. Worse than piss."

Roman laughed nervously. Mallon spoke his mind. Maybe that was the European side of him. "It's as good as it gets in here. The drinks have always been rough."

Mallon leaned closer and put a hand on Roman's wrist. The scent of his aftershave was intoxicating. Even the smoke and cheap whisky on his breath was attractive. "I don't want to stay here. Come to my hotel. I have liquor. We'll have a good drink then I'll fuck you, like I wanted to earlier."

Roman's heart was in his throat again. Not through fear this time, but animal attraction and desire. The touch of Mallon's hand, the closeness of his face, it was impossible to resist. "All right," he said.

Mallon leaned closer, his head tilted. When their lips met, Roman felt an electrical exchange between them. It went straight from his mouth to his groin.

He knew in that second that Mallon could ask anything of him tonight, and he would deliver.

Chapter Four

"A sweet taste of what's to come."

The Vermont Hotel had been a part of Roman's life for as long as he had lived in Blyham. As a student, he used to work seasonal shifts in their Michelin-starred restaurant and had covered tables at one of their many corporate events. These days, he could see it's majestic ten story structure from the other side of the river on his journey to and from work. But in all those years, he had not set foot inside one of the bedrooms...until tonight.

He had been surprised when Mallon told him where he was staying. From his laid-back attitude and street-fighting ways, he'd expected him to have a room in one of the budget chain hotels, of which Blyham had six, situated in all areas of the city. He should have known better than to judge a man by his appearance.

The Vermont stood out among the crowd of high-end bars, restaurants, shops and hotels that dominated Blyham's chic waterfront district. It was the jewel in a gentrified crown.

They arrived by Uber. No more taking chances on the dangerous streets. Mallon showed his room card to the twenty-four-hour concierge, and they crossed the marbled floor of the reception. There were still people drinking in the hotel's foyer bar. He knew there was another bar, on the roof terrace, though Roman doubted that would be serving at this hour.

They entered the lift alone, and Mallen pressed the button for the seventh floor.

As soon as the doors closed, he was on Roman. He grasped his head in both hands and kissed him. Roman was a few inches taller than Mallon, but the older man dominated him in every way, pushing him against the wall of the elevator and shoving his tongue into his mouth. Roman gripped his shoulders, surrendering as Mallon ground his bulge against his hips.

The passion of the kiss disarmed him. Roman's legs trembled as he thrust his tongue against Mallon's, experiencing the heat of his breath, the raspy contact of their stubbled skin. Few of the men he had met on a casual basis were into kissing. Many of them refused to do it, and those who did were often terrible. Not Mallon. This guy knew how to kiss and make it count.

Roman squirmed, grinding his hips against his cock, discerning its size and girth. It had been completely concealed by Cameron's greedy mouth in the club, and he had no idea what to expect, but from the way Mallon pressed it onto him, he would not be disappointed.

The doors open. Mallon slid a hand around Roman's waist and shoved it down the back of his jeans, cupping his arse. His fingers slithered into the sweaty crack. Roman caught a quick breath. This man was bold. He knew what he wanted and went for it. As they walked along the corridor, Mallon's fingertip found the hot opening, and traced the rim.

"Tonight, your ass is mine."

Roman nodded and licked his lips. His mouth was dry. "Yes. It's all yours."

"To do what I want with?"

"Anything." His insides tightened, and a fire of need burned in his butt like nothing he'd known.

They reached the door of his room. Mallon swiped the card, and they went inside.

It was more than a hotel room. There was a large seating area with a sofa, armchair and coffee table, and the bedroom was around an L-shaped bend. This had to be one of the junior suites. Roman had heard of them but didn't know what to expect. The décor was all cream, beige and gold, illuminated by multiple side lights strategically placed around the room. Whatever Mallon did for a living, whatever had brought him to Blyham, had to be worth a lot of money.

Mallon withdrew his hand from Roman's arse. He raised his fingers to this nose and sniffed, before grinning and sucking the tip.

"Mmm," Mallon said. "A sweet taste of what's to come."

He crossed to the seating area. He had a languid, sensual way of walking. Roman stared at the mounds of his buttocks in his tight jeans. There was a marble-topped bar in the corner. Mallon pulled forward two tumblers. There was a bottle of whisky on the top. He splashed a generous measure into one of the glasses before raising the bottle to Roman. "Eh?"

"Vodka, if you have any."

He opened the fridge beneath the bar and pulled out a couple of miniatures and Diet Cokes. "Help yourself," he said, moving to the armchair and sitting down. He crossed his ankle over his knee and reclined, sipping the whisky.

Roman showed his scuffed palms. "Mind if I use your bathroom first? To clean these up."

Mallon jerked his thumb. "That way."

Roman's breath was short and fast as he ran his hands under the tap. The bathroom was even posher than he'd expected. He smiled nervously at his reflection, not ready to believe any of this was happening.

Mallon was lounging in the armchair when he returned, looking sexier than ever.

Roman stumbled to the bar. *Why do I feel so self-conscious in front of him?* Mallon moved with the lythe grace of a cat. Roman was a clumsy puppy in comparison.

The vodka was Grey Goose. He emptied one of the miniatures into a glass and topped it up with the Coke, before taking a deep drink. "You were right," he said. "This is a lot better than what they serve at The New Inn."

Mallon shrugged. "What could be worse than that piss?"

Roman laughed nervously and took another drink.

Mallon's intense grey eyes were laser focused. Roman found it impossible to maintain contact with them.

"Do I make you uncomfortable?" Mallon asked.

"No," he said quickly. "It's not you. It's well...everything. This place is not what I'm used to, and it's been an unusual night already. I guess, I'm a little overwhelmed."

Mallon's face was deadly serious. "Still want to fuck? After all you've been through."

"Oh God, yes." Roman stepped forward. Did Mallon think he'd gone cold on the idea? Even worse, had Mallon gone cold on the idea. "That's what I'm here for."

Mallon's eyes narrowed. The moment was interminable as he weighed up the situation. At last, he gave a tiny nod and took another sip of whisky. "Take off your pants. Let me see your ass."

Roman's pulse quickened again. He set his drink on the coffee table and lifted his T-shirt.

"No," Mallon said, raising his hand. "Leave that on. Just your bottoms off. I want to see your ass, nothing else. And turn around."

Heat rushed to his face. *What kind of request is this?* It seemed so strange, and yet his cock was like an iron rod. He turned. It was suddenly easier with his back to Mallon, without that scrutinising stare. He stepped out of his Converse shoes and unfastened his jeans, shoving them to his ankles and stepping out, kicking them aside. He wore a pair of navy trunks. He paused for a moment, knowing how well they hugged his arse, before shoving them off completely and pulling his shoes back on. "Like this?" he asked, standing straight.

Silence from behind. His heart hammered against his ribs. *Is my arse not good enough for him?* For an otherwise slender guy, Roman knew his butt was on the chunky side. Did Mallon want something smaller? Perter? Tattooed? Like Cameron?

Mallon released a deep, guttural groan. "That ass is fucking perfect. Raise your T-shirt a little. Show me more."

Roman obeyed, gathered the hem of his shirt to expose his cheeks.

Mallon let out another appreciative groan and muttered something in a language Roman didn't understand. It sounded like French, but he couldn't be certain. He was used to posing. It was all part of the dating game. Guys on apps always asked him to show this or that, to bend in a certain way or spread his legs to their requirements. Roman could get himself into all kinds of positions to suit the needs of random strangers. At least with Mallon, he didn't have to factor in the angle of his camera. He leaned forward, widening his stance to show off more of his arse. He tilted his hips slowly from side to side. He'd edited enough of his own videos to know his butt looked good like that.

He glanced over his shoulder. Mallon was in the same position as before, his ankle crossed on his knee, as he nursed his drink and feasted his eyes.

Oh, yes. He likes it all right.

Roman spread his feet wider and opened his thighs, pushing his hard cock and balls down between his legs so Mallon could take it in, pole and hole all at once.

"Leave your dick," Mallon growled. "It's your pussy I'm interested in. Spread your ass and show me."

Roman had never been keen on men referring to his arse as a pussy, but he let it slide this one time. Mallon was so unbelievably hot that he could call him whatever the fuck he wanted. In that accent, everything sounded sexy.

He took a long breath and planted both of his hands on his cheeks. This is where things could go wrong. He'd been with men who were only interested in hairy arses and others who insisted on the complete back, crack and sack wax. Roman fell somewhere in-between. He used hair clippers to keep his body hair in check but had never been a fan of waxing or hair creams. It was time to show Mallon what he had. He spread his cheeks wide.

The moan from the armchair let him know the older man was happy with what he saw.

"Fantastic," Mallon said, before muttering something he didn't understand.

Roman's cock was at full mast. Exhibition was all part of life. If he didn't show off, no one would ever fuck him, but he'd never been particularly into that fetish. Tonight was different. Showing off to Mallon was the greatest turn-on.

"Get on the couch," Mallon told him. "On your knees, arms over the backrest, ass in the air."

Pre-cum oozed from the tip of Roman's cock and drooled down the shaft. He had barely touched his dick but was so aroused. He climbed onto the sofa and assumed the required position, resting his elbows along the back and sticking his butt out. He'd often felt self-conscious and stupid when performing sexy stuff like this before, but this made him feel super-hot. His entire body jangled with desire, desperate for Mallon to touch him, to pound his dumb brains out.

There was movement from the armchair behind, but he kept his gaze focused in front. He instinctively knew this was what Mallon wanted. He shuddered with anticipation was he heard the clink of the glass being put down on the table. *This is it*. He steadied himself. *He's going to take me.*

A hand moved along the curve of his back, from his shoulders down the length of his spine. Roman prickled with gooseflesh when Mallon's palm made contact with the bare skin of his arse. Mallon cupped his right buttock, squeezing gently, then stroking, caressing in slow, tender circles.

"That's a fine ass," Mallow whispered. "There wasn't another man in the club who could compete with you. I knew it the second I saw you, that I would have you."

Roman rested his forehead on his folded arms. He could listen to this all night. He didn't believe the part about being the hottest guy in the club, but for now, he could surrender to the fantasy. Mallon gripped his left cheek with his other hand. Roman pressed backwards, delivering his butt...then the stretch as Mallon parted and spread him. He felt the tautness of his anus as it broadened.

Roman shuddered when Mallon's wet tongue slithered along his crack, so light to begin, skirting around the sensitive rim, the most exquisite tickling sensation.

"Oh God," Roman groaned, closing his eyes and focusing all his attention on his arse. It was the best sensation in the world. Too many men refused to lick another man's hole, and of the ones who did, so few of them had any idea what they were doing. Roman was certain a man had to love having his own hole eaten in order to know how to do it, to know what made it so good.

He heard Mallon chuckle. "I've found your sweet spot. Now let me get your pussy wet and loose. I know what you're going to like."

It was no lie or exaggeration. Roman squirmed with delight as Mallon's expert tongue wriggled around his hole and sent surges of pleasure through his body. Mallon gripped his hips in both hands and pulled

Roman's arse against his face. The tip of his tongue flickered across the opening and traced wet lines around the rim. His arsehole pulsed, greedy for even more. Roman sighed and moaned. He'd never felt so intimate with a man, and they hadn't even fucked yet. If Mallon could reduce him to a quivering wreck with just his tongue, what would his cock be capable of?

He had no sense of time or how long Mallon ate his arse. Roman was lost to the warm, moist heat of that mouth against his hole. This had become his most intense sexual experience since the night when he had lost his virginity.

Except this was even better. Unlike the lad who had taken his cherry, Mallon knew what he was doing.

Mallon withdrew and gave his butt a gentle, open-handed slap. "Stay right there. It's time to fuck."

Roman watched over his shoulder as Mallon stood and undressed.

"You want me to wear a condom?" Mallon asked.

"I'm on PrEP," Roman answered.

Mallon grinned. With his wide mouth and dimples, it was devastatingly sexy. "Me too. Then we're both good."

In just his underpants, he hurried to the bedroom, returning moments later with a small bottle of lube. He stood over Roman from behind and drizzled the cool liquid from a height. Roman gasped as it ran down his arse crack, then Mallon's fingers were in there, pushing, probing, going deep inside to prepare the way. He dropped his underpants, and Roman heard the slick sound of him fisting lube over his cock. Then Mallon's hands were on his waist and his wet cockhead bumped his hole.

Roman had no idea what to expect. He still hadn't seen Mallon's dick, but he didn't care. He was ready for whatever was about to happen. He pushed back against the blunt crown. His hole stretched, desperate to have it. Mallon chuckled. "You're a greedy boy."

Roman nodded. "Fuck me," he pleaded.

Mallon gripped his hips tighter and leaned into him. The stretch made Roman open his mouth and eyes at the same time. *Holy shit.* Wider, wider. He gasped. The head still was not inside him. *He's going to break me.*

They both groaned as Mallon destroyed the resistance of his sphincter. Once through, the rest of his shaft slipped in easily until his hips pressed against Roman's buttocks. Roman breathed deeply, adjusting to the intrusion. He was used to cocks of all sizes and shapes, but this one took some getting used to.

Mallon twitched and throbbed inside him. "It's what you wanted. Yes?"

Roman signed and closed his eyes. "Yes. I want it."

Mallon gripped the back of his T-shirt and twisted tight, using it like a rein, and eased his cock back, leaving just the head inside. He paused, teasing, waiting until Roman was on the verge of begging, before sliding it all the way back in to the hilt. They both groaned once it was buried deep. Mallon took up a slow and gentle pace, letting Roman appreciate every thick, meaty inch of his dick.

Roman was so used to casual hook-ups who jumped on and fucked hard and fast before finishing in a few minutes, that this was something new. Mallon fucked his arse as expertly as he had eaten it, ensuring maximum pleasure. *Why can't all tops be this good?*

After a good ten minutes of leisurely fucking, Mallon withdrew and tapped his butt. "On your back," he demanded.

Roman rolled over and down. Mallon grabbed his ankles, hauled his arse to the edge of the sofa and held his legs high and wide, before slipping back inside. Roman's arse was so wet and relaxed that he entered him effortlessly. This new position was even better, allowing Roman to look at Mallon's face while he fucked him. Mallon let go of his ankles, leaned on top of him, gripping his arse to go deeper. The position brought his cock into perfect alignment with Roman's prostate, taking him to an even greater state of bliss. Roman wrapped his legs around Mallon's waist and grabbed his shoulders, locking him in tight.

This was more than sex, more than a random shag. This was everything.

Mallon's body was on fire. Sweat made his skin slick to touch. Roman buried his face into his shoulder, kissing and tasting the saltiness. Mallon's cock pounded directly against his prostate again and again in a sublime rhythm, sending a rush all through his body. He couldn't believe what was happening as the sensations intensified.

"Oh God...I think I'm coming..."

His breath became deeper and more ragged. Without touching his cock, he was about to blow. Mallon fucked him with deeper determination, driving pulses of pleasure through his pelvis.

"Oh shit." Roman's legs tightened around Mallon's waist as he came. Powerful beats ran through his core, his balls, all along his cock, ending with wet surges across his belly — one after another after another. The orgasm was deep and prolonged, and as his arsehole tightened and gripped Mallon's cock, it took him, too. Mallon let out a roar, burying his head into Roman's neck and clutching his arse as he emptied his load inside him.

They remained in position afterwards…too shook, too stunned to move. Mallon's heart beat a rapid tattoo against Roman's chest, and his breath was ragged against his skin. Roman's head was in another place on a high, a plateau of ecstasy.

It would take him a long time to come down.

Chapter Five

The Morning After

In the morning, Roman was gently wakened by a firm hand caressing his abdomen from behind. He lay on his side in the luxurious bed with his back pressed against Mallon's chest. Mallon's warm lips brushed his neck. Roman moaned to let his lover know he was awake. Without further promoting, Mallon's hand moved lower to grasp Roman's cock. He squeezed the hard shaft before moving to the tip and rubbing his thumb over the folds of foreskin, which were already wet with pre-cum.

Roman sighed and rolled onto his back. It was all the encouragement the older man needed. He moved between Roman's legs and lifted his hips until they were in his lap. When Mallon's cock bounced against his arse, Roman adjusted position, finding the head with his hole and pushing downwards. Mallon slipped in effortlessly, and they were joined again. It was a steady morning fuck. Roman ground his hips upon Mallon, watching his face for signs of orgasm. When Mallon's brow furrowed and his lips tightened, Roman gripped his own cock. All it took was a gentle touch, and he timed it perfectly, splattering his belly with cum while Mallon filled his insides.

They collapsed side by side afterwards, smiling as they caught their breaths. Roman squeezed his arse, loving the used, wet feel of his usually tight hole. He reached between his thighs to touch it, loving how warm it was and slightly sore. Some of Mallon's cum leaked onto his fingers as he touched it.

"I'm glad I found you," Mallon said, gazing at the ceiling, one arm flung behind his head. "You must be the best bottom in Blyham."

Roman laughed. "I think a lot of men would lay claim to that crown and be highly offended to know you said otherwise." He rolled onto his side and propped himself on an elbow, to better look at him. "We're a good fit. I think that's what made it work so well."

He ran his hand across Mallon's chest and stomach. Like Roman, he had manscaped his body hair to a light coating. He even had a neat pubic bush — a rare find in an era of fully shaven groins. Roman let his hand drift lower, grazing his fingertips across Mallon's softening cock. The fine skin was still sticky from his arse. Mallon was circumcised. Roman hadn't encountered many men who were cut, but Mallon's was neater and better done than the others he had seen. He traced his finger around the head. Mallon jerked involuntarily.

"Sorry," Roman said, drawing away.

"It's sensitive, that's all." Mallon's eyes were closed, his face still turned to the ceiling.

Roman squinted at his watch in the dull light. It was nearly eleven. Later than he'd thought, but then again, when had they fallen asleep? It must have been close to five, if not later. After fucking him on the sofa, they had finished their drinks before coming into the bedroom, where Mallon's had eaten his arse all over again before fucking him face down.

No wonder my hole is leaking. He's left three loads in there.

"Will you be here for long?" he asked. "In Blyham, I mean."

"Not this time. I'm leaving tomorrow." He rolled over to look at his watch on the bedside. "We need to move. I have work to do." He leapt out of bed and bounded to the window, pulling open the curtains, giving Roman a nice view of his chunky arse.

Roman hid his disappointment at the news. He'd have liked the chance to test his theory about Mallon's rimming skills by burying his face in there and seeing how much he liked it. "Do you mind if I use your shower before I leave?"

"Go ahead. You know where it is. I'll order breakfast. Coffee? Croissants?"

"Tea, please...if that's okay."

Mallon didn't even look at him as he strode naked into the living room and picked up the phone.

Oh, well. At least I got to spend the night. Mallon wasn't one of those guys who couldn't wait to run once they'd shot their load.

The shower was filled with expensive bottles of shampoo and body wash. Roman took his time beneath the powerful jets, washing his hair and cleaning the cum from his stomach and butt crack. It was only then that he noticed the pain in his abdomen and lower back and as he looked closer, he saw the flesh was already blooming into dark blue and purple bruises. He had been so turned by sex with Mallon that he'd completely forgotten about the attack. *Jesus*. Those bastards had hit him hard to cause such damage. Adrenaline must have dulled the worst of the pain.

He dried off carefully and helped himself to Mallon's deodorant — another expensive-smelling brand he did not recognise.

Mallon was sitting on the sofa in a white robe when Roman came out of the bathroom with a towel around his waist. He searched the room for his clothes, which had been discarded in a passionate rush. He found his shoes first then his T-shirt.

"Are you going to the police?" Mallon asked, staring at the bruises on Roman's torso.

"There's no point. You dealt with the problem."

"Until they do it again. You heard what they said. They'll be back, and the next man might not be so lucky. You should report it, at least."

"It won't make any difference. People have been attacked and beaten up much worse than this in the last year. Five men are dead. How many police did you see on the streets last night? None, right? Because there aren't any. They have done sweet-fuck-all to protect the community, despite everything that's happened. We don't matter. We're just a bunch of queers. They won't do a thing to look for the men who attacked me. Nothing."

Mallon's brow furrowed. "Then you need to learn to fight. Boxing. Judo. Take up some kind of self-defence so you can retaliate next time."

"I don't think there will be a next time. From now on, I won't be so stupid as to walk around alone at night."

Mallon's mouth turned down. "You will. You'll forget your fear in a week, maybe two, and you'll find yourself in the same situation, wandering around, putting your life at risk to find another dick."

* * * *

After their quick breakfast, Mallon made it clear that it was time for Roman to go.

He had managed to discover that Mallon lived in Lyon, France, but not the nature of his business in Blyham.

"Will you be back here soon?" he asked, unable to keep the note of hopeful desperation from his voice as Mallon edged him towards the door.

Mallon shrugged. "It's likely."

"How soon?"

"I have no idea. I travel a lot, rarely with much notice."

"Would you like to exchange numbers? So we can keep in touch?"

Mallon shook his head. "Not a good idea."

His words stung, but Roman hid the hurt behind a plastered smile. "That's cool."

"Maybe we'll run into each other another time, but I don't like to make promises or commit myself." He opened the door.

Time's up.

"I hope we do," Roman stalled. "It was great meeting you. Well, more than great. I owe you a lot."

Mallon's face clouded with impatience. "Yes. Now, I really do have work."

Roman realised the French man had no intention of kissing him, so leaned in fast and pressed his lips to Mallon's closed mouth.

At last Mallon smiled. "You're a handful, you know? You're a lovely boy. I hope you find who you are looking for. In the meantime, be careful. Now that you know how dangerous it is out there, don't get caught again."

The door closed behind him. Regret consumed Roman all the way to the elevator. He might never see this man again. *What a shame.* Mallon was perfect for him in every way. *Aloof, sure, and closed off, but damn, he was a sexy fucker.* Roman might spend the rest of the year comparing every man he met to Mallon. He doubted anyone would fuck him that good again. After so many hollow sexual encounters, he'd finally experienced a deeper, more primal connection...with a man who lived in another country and was going home tomorrow.

By the time he reached the lobby, his regret had turned to gratitude. He might not see Mallon again, but they had shared a special night. Roman wouldn't forget it in a hurry. He couldn't say that about many of his hook-ups. The French man had left an indelible mark on his psyche.

It was a decent morning when he came out of the hotel. The sky was filled with low, grey clouds, but it was mild for the time of year. He decided to save some cash and walk home, setting out along the waterfront. It was approaching midday, and the bars and restaurants were open, geared up for their busy Saturday trade. In another hour they would be filled with the stag and hen parties that flocked to Blyham each weekend, tottering from venue to venue in their bridal veils, drinking cocktails through penis-shaped straws. Many of the loftier establishments refused entry to the party crowds, but there were enough places willing to accept them and the chaos they brought to keep them coming to the city. Roman avoided the area at the weekend, but it was early enough for him to feel safe.

He was at less risk here than the supposed secure haven of the village these days.

Since his rescue by Mallon, he'd given little thought to what had happened. Mallon had made him feel safe, protected then desired. There was nothing to fear when they were together. He wondered if the anger would hit him later. Maybe Mallon was right, and he should report the incident to the cops.

He doubted they would do much, other than add it to their statistic sheet, but maybe that was better than nothing. The more attacks that were reported, the more obvious the problem would become, so obvious they might get their fingers out of their arses and do something to protect the community.

Fat fucking chance.

If nothing else, his report might inconvenience some police officer for half an hour. That alone must make it worth doing.

Gazing at the terraces of the café bars, he imagined what it would be like to sit there and enjoy a waterfront brunch or a drink with Mallon—like a scene from a glamourous movie, not a romcom. Mallon was far too serious for that. A sexy drama, or an intense thriller… They could be undercover agents…or men from different sides meeting to exchange information.

He smiled as he walked. Mallon was having an odd effect on him. Roman didn't romanticise the man he slept with. In most cases he didn't give them another thought. Why should Mallon be different? He'd struck at something deep within him.

Even deeper than his cock had gone.

Roman's grin widened farther. He'd been reluctant to take that shower earlier. He'd have liked to walk home with the scent of Mallon still on him, but he'd sweated so much with every fuck, he would stink too bad. If he squeezed his hole, it was easy to remember the feel of him in there. His arse was still tender and a little loose after all that action, and he had three loads of cum up there. Mallon's cum.

When he got home, he could lie back and finger himself, unleashing some of that sperm. He could have a wank while the memory of the man was fresh, like he hadn't had enough sex already.

I doubt I'd ever have enough of him.

Roman realised he was completely smitten. It was a good thing that Mallon was going away, because if he stayed, the temptation to pursue him and do it all again would be too great. He would no longer be a rational man, just someone ruled by his cock and his hole.

On the dangerous streets of Blyham, that was not a good prospect.

Chapter Six

Saturday Night's Alright for Fighting

Roman couldn't afford to go out two nights in a row, but when his flatmate Ashley suggested a few beers in the village, he jumped at the chance. Mallon had said he was leaving the next day, but there was a chance — a slim one — that he might be in one of the bars that evening. He had been noncommittal about seeing Roman again, but Roman was certain if Mallon saw him, he would not be able to resist.

Ashley had other ideas. "You can't let what those bastards did to you last night scare you off. You need to get out as soon as possible and overcome your fear."

Roman was not afraid. The men who had attacked him were opportunistic bullies. He had been in the wrong place at the wrong time when they'd come along. The stupid bastards had gotten more than they had reckoned for and would seek an easier target next time, he was sure of that. It was the hope of seeing Mallon that drew him back to the village, rather than a need to overcome any trauma relating to the assault.

He took time getting ready, lingering in the bathtub for an hour to ease the tenderness in his torso. His assailants had struck a couple of powerful blows before his hero had arrived, and Roman was starting to suffer the consequences. He put on a pair of his favourite boxer-briefs, the ones he saved for hook-ups when a good fuck was guaranteed. Mallon had seemed so into his arse last night, worshipping with his eyes and tongue. He wouldn't be able to resist Roman in this pair of underpants. Fresh jeans and his favourite blue shirt completed the look. The weather had taken a cold turn, and he had to make a last-minute addition of a jacket before leaving the flat.

They took an Uber into the city centre, and Roman was disappointed when they ran into Ashley's prick boyfriend Patrick in the first bar they visited.

"You didn't tell me he was coming."

"Why wouldn't he be here? He is my boyfriend. It's what couples do on Saturday nights," Ashley said defensively. "They go out together."

As long as that's all they did. Ashey and Patrick had a habit of starting arguments and fights when they had both been drinking. They couldn't seem to help themselves. With Patrick along, this would not be the fun evening Ashley had promised him.

If he found Mallon that wouldn't matter. Roman would ditch them the first chance he got.

They started at The New Inn, which was far busier than when he had been here last night. While he waited for Ashley to order their drinks, he scanned the crowd in the bar and the terrace. The resident DJ played a selection of camp classics, though it was difficult to hear the songs over the loud conversations. How likely was he to find Mallon here? Not at all, after the French man's comments on the quality of the drinks, but it did not keep him from looking. Roman was an optimist.

He spotted Cameron, the slutty twink who had sucked off Mallon at the club. He held court on the terrace with a group of his party friends, cackling as they smoked and vaped. Despite the cool night, he wore a skimpy white T-shirt and low-riding jeans that revealed the waist band of his jock and an inch of butt crack. Roman grimaced and wondered what Mallon had found so attractive about him. Not much, he reminded himself. After a toothy blow job, Mallon had ditched Cameron to seek him out instead. That's all he needed to know. Still, Cameron was persistent. If he ran into Mallon tonight, he would take another shot.

"Who are you looking for?" Ashley asked when he brought their drinks over. *Two beers.* Far safer than the awful house spirits.

"I hoped I might see the guy from last night, to let him know what the police said today."

"Didn't you get his number? Text him."

Roman shook his head. "He didn't give it to me."

"Probably married, then."

"What makes you say that?"

"Rich businessman, away from home. It's classic. He'll have a wife and a couple of kids in France who have no idea he likes to stick it to other men."

Roman hid his irritation. "Not all men are the same. He didn't seem the type. Besides, no straight man could fuck another guy the way he fucked me."

Ashley guffawed and rolled his eyes. "Did I say he was straight? Lots of men identify as bisexual these days. It doesn't mean he doesn't have a family tucked away." He swigged his beer. "You were just an easy mouth and open hole for the night. Accept it and get over it."

Roman bit his tongue. Just because Patrick couldn't be faithful for more than a couple of weeks, it didn't mean all men were the same. Patrick treated Ashley like shit, and Roman was always there to support him afterwards. The least he could do now was return the favour.

From The New Inn they moved to Julie's. To Roman's relief, Patrick met up with one of his drug buddies and fell behind.

"What's he taking now?" Roman asked as they hurried to the next venue. After the assault, he wasn't keen to spend too much time on the streets.

"Nothing," Ashley said. "That's what he told me, anyway."

"Don't tell me you believe him?"

Ashley sighed. "Of course not. Just because I love him, it doesn't make me an idiot. He's still using steroids, though he doesn't really count those. He classes them as supplements."

"What else?"

"Judging by the look in his eyes tonight, he's taken speed or coke already."

Roman put an arm around Ashley's shoulder. His friend had his faults, but he had always been very anti-drugs. He'd cut ties with previous mates in the past when their partying ways had gotten out of hand. Roman had never understood why he made exceptions for Patrick. It wasn't like Patrick was even that hot. Roman found his ballooning biceps and bulging veins repulsive. Ashley had dated far sexier guys than him, men who were more worthy of his affection than that meathead.

"Why do you put up with him?" Roman asked.

"Look… I know you don't like him —"

"That's an understatement. He treats you like shit and thinks I'm even worse than that. I can't stand the man."

"But I love him. I can't explain why, but I do. You must accept that."

Roman squeezed him caringly. "I accept you have the worst taste and judgement in men of anyone I know, but I put up with him, don't I? For your sake."

Ashley laughed and leaned into him. "You say that like you didn't hook up with a married businessman last night, the oldest cliché in the book."

"Let's agree to disagree about men, eh? At least for tonight."

At Julie's, Roman queued at the bar to get the next round of drinks. As he waited to make payment, the manager Phil spotted him and came out from behind the counter.

"Are you all right? I heard what happened."

Roman raised his shirt to display the bruises, which had spread and turned a dark shade of purple. "They look worse than they are."

"Oh my God. What were you thinking?" Phil gathered him to his chest and hugged him gently. "Did it really happen after you left here?"

Roman nodded. "Just up the road. I was looking for a taxi when they jumped me."

"Why didn't you say something? I could have called you a cab. You didn't have you go out there by yourself."

"It's fine, really. I didn't think I needed one. They took me by surprise, that's all."

"They could have killed you—or given you a lot more to worry about than a couple of bruises." Phil told him to put his debit card away. "Your drinks are on the house tonight. It's the least we can do for you. What about the police? Please tell me you reported this."

"It's okay, I did. I spoke to them this afternoon."

"And? What did they say? Did they take photos of your injuries?"

"They haven't even seen them. I gave my statement over the phone. They've given me an incident number, and I suspect that's as far as it will go."

Phil's jaw dropped. "You're fucking kidding. Another major assault in the village, and they do fuck all about it. This is outrageous. How many more people need to be attacked? How many have to die before they give a shit?"

Roman nodded. He shared the older man's anger and exasperation, but if the police wouldn't do anything, he didn't see how they could change that. "This guy came along and helped me." He told him about Mallon. "You should have seen him. He was like someone from a Marvel movie. He took down all three of them."

"Then you're bloody lucky. You might not be the next time."

A group of overexcited young women pushed to the bar, giggling and screaming. Roman and Phil stepped aside to give them room. Phil pulled a packet of cigarettes from the pocket of his apron and indicated they should go outside. The beer garden was busy but quieter and cooler than the interior.

"We need to do something about this," Phil said. "The police are useless, the press doesn't even report these attacks anymore, and we need to take matters into our own hands."

"What are you suggesting? A vigilante group?"

Phil shook his head. "That's not my way of working. That will only make matters worse. The homophobes will see it as a challenge to come down here and fight the gays. But if no one will listen to us, we need to make more noise. Rallies, petitions, we need to march on the town and make sure the news cameras are there to see it."

Roman said nothing. He didn't share the militant spirit of a lot of the older people in the community. They loved a loud protest. He preferred to keep his head down and avoid confrontation, not that it had worked too well for him last night. "I wondered whether you knew the guy who stepped in to help me?" he said, changing the direction of their conversation.

"Who was he?"

"A French guy called Mallon. He said he's here on business, but it's not the first time. I got the impression he's here quite often."

Phil shook his head, drawing on his cigarette. "Doesn't ring a bell."

"He'd be in his mid-thirties, dark hair, really startling grey eyes — square jawed, handsome."

Phil exhaled smoke. "Kind of intense-looking? Miserable even?"

Roman perked up. "That sounds like him."

"I didn't know his name, but that sounds a like a bloke who has been in here a few times. Not really a regular. There must be weeks, if not months between his visits. In fact, I can't remember when I last saw him.

It's been a while. He keeps to himself. He's the one who kicked the arses of your attackers?"

"Yes. He did."

Phil smiled and nodded. "Impressive. I wouldn't have thought he had it in him. He's not the biggest bloke, is he?" He mimed flexing his muscles.

"No, but he was strong."

"Must be." Phil took another drag on his cigarette, scratched his beard then said, "Oh, hang on. I do remember him." He laughed. "He went home with Tyler one time last year. It must have been around Christmas."

Roman stiffened as a coil of jealously wrapped around his insides. "Tyler?"

"You know, Tyler, the security guard. He's on the door tonight. You'll have passed him to get in."

The coil tightened. Tyler the door attendant was a walking mountain of muscle and attitude. With his buzzed haircut and steroid-boosted physique, he came from the same body-builder mould as Patrick. *Mallon is into guys like that. First a trashy queen like Cameron and now this.*

"Yeah, I remember," he laughed harder. "Tyler could barely sit down for a week afterwards. He said the French guy fucked him so hard he thought his teeth would drop out. For a big guy, Tyler got a lot more than he bargained for. No wonder those three last night came off second best. This guy Mallon must be deceptively physical."

* * * *

Roman and Ashley were in the beer garden enjoying their third drink and having a laugh when Patrick caught up with them. He barged through the crowd, shoving a young couple aside without a glance. Roman only had to look at him to know trouble was coming. His eyes were bloodshot, and the pupils constricted. His bullish face was set in a mean expression he was already familiar with.

"The fuck you doing here?" he snapped at Ashley. "We're supposed to be going to Sash."

"I'm enjoying myself here," Ashley said. Roman detected the defensive tone that was a familiar precursor to one of their fights. He felt his friend go taut in a defensive stance. "The music and atmosphere are much better."

Patrick's nostrils flared. "It's crap. The music is shit in here. C'mon. We're going to Sash." He grabbed Ashley's wrist.

The bastard needed to score. The real hardcore drug dealers of Blyham hung around Sash. Phil and his team kept them out of Julie's.

"There's no one stopping you," Roman interjected. "You don't need us to hold your hand."

Emboldened, Ashley snatched his wrist away. "That's right. Go and do your own thing. You usually do anyway."

Patrick stepped closer, puffing out his over-inflated chest. "Stop being a cunt. You're coming with me."

Roman controlled the urge to butt in again. This would go one of two ways. Ashley would back down and concede to his bullying boyfriend, or he would stand up to him and a public slanging match would ensue. Roman was in no mood for either option, but he would back his friend all the way.

"Don't call me that," Ashley said, moving closer to Roman and distancing himself from Patrick.

A vein in Patrick's throat throbbed. "It's what you are...a bitchy little cunt. You and your girlfriend. The pair of you are as bad as each other."

Roman couldn't contain himself. "Have the steroids shrivelled your brain as well as your cock? Fuck off back to Sash with the rest of the tweakers and leave us alone. We were having a nice time until you arrived and spoiled it."

For the second time in less than twenty-four-hours Roman found himself on the receiving end of a punch from a much bigger man. Patrick's fist lacked the force and intent of the man who had attacked him on the street, but it landed in his belly with enough power to wind him. He staggered backwards, more surprised than hurt.

There was an eruption of noise around him, angry protests from those who had witnessed the assault. They surrounded and protected him as a group, while a glass of beer was dumped over Patrick's head. He stood there, gawping as it gushed down his face and neck.

Before Patrick could react further, Phil and Tyler, the colossal door attendant, appeared. Tyler took Patrick from behind, twisting his arm behind his back.

"Let go of me, you cunt," Patrick snarled.

"Out," Phil snapped. "And don't come back. You're barred, for good. We've got enough trouble on the streets without the likes of you kicking off inside."

Another bouncer appeared, and together with Tyler, they hauled Patrick to the exit. He twisted and snarled in their grip, kicking at their legs, but they carried him effortlessly to the door.

"Oh my God," Ashley gasped, rounding on Roman. "Are you all right? I can't believe he hit you." Ashley's face was slack with shock.

"I can," Roman said bitterly. The walls in their flat were thin, and he'd heard more than once how Ashley's rows with Patrick could descend into violence. "I think the ban on Patrick needs to extend to our home. He's trouble, and neither of us needs it."

Ashley nodded numbly. "Sure," he said. "He's out."

Roman didn't believe him. He had forgiven Patrick for worse than this.

Phil came over. "Twice in two days. You're becoming a magnet for trouble. Are you all right?"

"I'm fine," Roman assured him and the concerned on-lookers. "For a big guy, there was no force to the punch."

"That's not the point," Phil said. "We caught the whole incident on our security camera." He turned on Ashley. "Tell your boyfriend I'm reporting this to the police as well the community newspapers. And I'll show the footage to every bar and restaurant manager in the area. He'll be banned from all of them by this time tomorrow. Count on it."

Ashley gulped. "Okay."

"He's a piece of shit. Do yourself a favour and get rid of him." With a final look of concern for Roman, Phil left them alone.

"Saturday night's alright for fighting," Roman said humourlessly.

"I...I... I don't..." Ashley's lips trembled.

"Don't try to defend him." Roman eased himself into a chair. Now the shock was wearing off, his legs trembled.

"I'm not," Ashley assured him. "I won't. Not after that. It's just...I can't believe he did that. That he hit you."

"But it's all right for him to hit you?" Roman said softly. "Just not anyone else."

Ashley's face turned red. He sat down with a long exhalation. "I didn't think you knew."

"In a two-bedroom flat... Do you think I'm deaf as well as stupid?" Roman swigged his beer. "I've never understood what you see in him. He's ugly, inside and out."

Ashley put his fist to his mouth. "It's over now. It really is. I can't make excuses for him anymore."

Roman moved closer and put his hand on his friend's arm. He spoke soft and gently. "You deserve better. Now that you're rid of him, you're going to find it."

There were tears in Ashley's eyes. He bit his knuckle, holding them at bay.

"Come on," Roman said. "Let's go home. I've had enough of these bars and being used as a punching bag for one weekend."

They both laughed. Ashley wiped his eyes. "Okay."

"Let's get a pizza. And a bottle of red wine from the all-nighter. It sounds a lot less dangerous than hanging around here, don't you think?" Roman said.

"Absolutely. Let's go."

* * * *

The taxi came to a stop in front of the three-storey terraced house. Two men got out of the back seat. Roman and his flat mate, Ashley.

From the other side of the road, in the alley between two houses, a figure, dressed head to toe in black, watched them.

There was muted laugher as they paid the taxi fare. Roman held a large pizza box while Ashley searched his pockets for keys. From a distance, the watcher could not catch what they said to each other as they climbed the steps to the front door, but there was more laughter and merriment. They were obviously having a good time.

They went inside, and a few minutes later a light came on in one of the second-floor windows. *The living room*. The watcher knew the layout of the flat, how the living room led to a small kitchen at the back. The two bedrooms were situated off the front door with a shared bathroom. Roman had the smaller of the rooms, the one that faced the rear of the house. The watcher knew everything.

What brought them home so early? The flatmate usually went out every Saturday night and never returned before three. Roman was less predictable. Some weeks he went out, others he stayed home, making use of the empty flat to entertain his endless hook-ups.

Something was different tonight, and that wouldn't do. It had to be a typical Saturday for this to work.

After another minute, the watcher faded into the shadows and disappeared through the alley that led to the next street.

The time would come. And soon. But it would not be tonight.

Chapter Seven

Murder with the Morning

Roman dreamed about Mallon. He was in bed with the hot French man, their limbs entwined, bodies arching together as they kissed and caressed every part of each other. Several times Roman threatened to wake up, but somehow forced himself back into the dream, where they were still together, still kissing, but fucking now. Roman moaned in his sleep. The dream was so real, so intense, that he could feel the heat of Mallon's body against his own, could smell his skin and taste the whisky and smoke on his breath.

An urgent knock at the bedroom door pulled him back to reality. He fought it, wanting to remain in his imagination with Mallon, but the knocking persisted and in seconds he was fully awake.

"What?" he groaned.

"Can I come in?" Ashley called.

Roman had tossed the covers aside in his sleep. A raging boner tented the front of his underpants. He grabbed the duvet and pulled it over him. "Okay." He rearranged the pillows and shuffled up the bed. *Ouch.* His head hurt when he moved.

They had gotten home before eleven and had polished off a full bottle of red wine with their pizza, before starting on a bottle of vodka and playing their favourite songs on YouTube as they opened their hearts to each other. Roman had admitted how strong the sexual desire Mallon had unleashed in him was, while Ashley got maudlin and detailed all the things he regretted about dating Patrick. He had a vague memory of stumbling to bed sometime after four.

Ashley came into the bedroom, wearing a pair of pyjama shorts and a baggy Spiderman T-shirt. He held his phone in front of him.

"What time is it?" Roman asked, shielding his eyes from light that came through the open door.

"Nearly one."

Shit. Another Sunday wasted to a late night and a hangover.

Roman groaned and wriggled into a sitting position. Ashley got onto the edge of the bed.

"Have you seen what's happened?" he asked.

"You've literally just woke me up," Roman laughed, managing to open his eyes fully for the first time. His Mallon-induced erection stayed rock hard beneath the covers.

"There's been another murder, someone from the village."

"What? Who?"

"Not sure. The victim lives on the Grange Estate in the East End, they say."

"How do you know it's related to the other killings?"

"It's what people are saying on WhatsApp and Facebook."

"Gossiping. It could be totally unconnected."

"They've never been wrong before." Ashley's WhatsApp group had broken the news of the last three murders in the community before the details had been publicly released. He tapped the screen of his phone as the messages refreshed. "It's definitely a murder. The police have got the whole place sealed off. Look."

He showed the screen, which displayed a photo of a typical crime scene. The area was taped and guarded by uniformed officers, while a fully kitted forensic team worked in the background. The horrible reality of the image shocked him wide-awake. Had another member of their community fallen victim to a hate crime?

"How long has it been since the last one?"

Ashley rubbed his stubbled chin. "About four months, give or take. Wasn't Charles Lear killed sometime in June? And that couple were killed a couple of months before that."

Roman nodded. "Yeah. That was in April, around Easter. Fuck. What is this city coming to?"

Ashley studied the photograph again. "The fucking police are only interested when someone gets killed, a juicy case they can cover themselves in glory with when they solve it. But if they do confirm the victim was one of us, no doubt they'll file it away and move on."

There was a huge distrust of Blyham Police with the LGBTQ community. Sometimes Roman thought his friends went too far in the fervour of their hatred of the cops, but he only had to remember the statistics to share their anger. Despite an overall rise in abuse and violence within the village, a figure he was now part of, five men had had been murdered in the last fourteen months and not a single charge had been brought. Several people had been arrested and taken in for questioning, friends and partners of the victims, but no serious suspects had come to light. If the current speculation was proved to be right, then this morning brought the total of dead to six — six that they knew of. There could be other deaths that hadn't been connected to the case.

Roman got wearily out of bed. He showered, feeling the full weight of the news, together with a thick hangover, and dressed in jeans and a comfortable, oversized sweater. After a couple of painkillers and a glass of juice, he started to feel more human. He made a pot of tea and searched the fridge and cupboard for something he could have for lunch. What he really would have liked was a slice of last night's pizza, all cold and stiff, but they had finished the lot in one sitting.

He opted for a tin of chicken soup, perfect comfort food for a grim day like this one. He emptied the can into a jug and put it in the microwave. Ashley rushed through from the living room, still in his bed wear, clutching his phone.

"You are not going to believe this," he said, pacing the kitchen.

Roman slumped against the counter. He didn't have the appetite for more bad news. Ashley was enjoying the drama.

"Just tell me.

"The guy who got killed last night. They're saying it's Cameron Taylor."

"Cameron Taylor?"

"Cameron. *'Fuck Me Cameron'*. The guy you said almost nixed your plans with the French guy in The Viaduct."

Roman heard what he was saying, but it took his mind a few seconds to compute and make sense of the words. *Cameron*. "Shit. Are you sure?"

Ashley brandished the phone. "They have never been wrong yet. That's his flat that the police are crawling all over."

Roman took a deep breath. He heard his blood pounding in his head. "But...I saw him last night. He was in The New Inn when we were there, out on the back terrace."

"Did you talk to him?"

"No. I doubt I've ever said more than a few words to him." Though Roman and Cameron had frequented all the same places for years, they had always maintained a distance, rivals who didn't dare get too close to each other. "He was with a group of other people."

"I didn't see him, though I didn't go out the back. I almost slept with him once, but neither of us were that into each other. Poor kid. I can't believe he is dead."

"Nor can I." Roman stared at his feet for several minutes. Though he could hardly say he had been close to Cameron, he was the first of the six victims he knew in a personal way. It brought the crisis closer to home than any of the others. "And his death is connected to the others? It's not some unrelated tragedy?"

"Too early to say, but it looks that way."

The facts of the previous murders were chillingly similar. Each of the victims had been found at home, naked in bed, with their bodies positioned in a grotesque parody of welcome, with arms and legs open. All five of the men had been strangled and sexually assaulted, though no trace of the killers DNA had been recovered. Many speculated that the sexual assaults had been carried out with a sex toy rather than a penis, leading to much speculation about the killer's motives. Some said he was a sexual oddball, destroying the men he desired and was unable to have for himself. Others insisted the murderer had to be a homophobe, using a dildo to violate the victims and make the killings look like the work of another gay guy. Everyone had a hypothesis for the murders, but no one had an answer.

And while everyone had been guessing, the killer had struck again.

* * * *

"How many more men have to die before anyone but us gives a damn?"

Phil's face was red with fury as he stubbed out a cigarette and immediately lit another.

The beer garden of Julie's was full. The news of Cameron's murder had brought the community out to mourn, and soon an informal meeting had begun as residents expressed their sadness for the young man's death and anger that it had happened again.

Roman and Ashley had been among the first to arrive around five o'clock. Neither of them were regulars on Sunday, but they had felt so restless at home, following the WhatsApp feed as more details were shared, that they had both felt an overwhelming need to get out and be part of the community. Roman had needed to receive support, and he wanted to give it back.

There was no doubt now that Cameron had become the sixth victim of what people in the pub were now calling 'The Blyham Strangler'. Cameron had lived alone in a small flat on a six-storey block. He'd been due to meet a friend for brunch that morning. When his friend couldn't get in touch with him, he had gone to the flat, let himself in and found Cameron laid out on the bed like the all the previous victims.

The police had still to release details to the press, but the news had already spread far.

As he sat at a crowded table, Roman couldn't stop thinking about Mallon and feeling guilty for it. Mallon wouldn't know what had happened to the boy he had almost spent the night with instead of Roman — the boy who had sucked his cock, regardless. Would he want to know? Would he care? He couldn't stop turning the questions over in his mind, and he hated himself for it. Mallon wasn't here. Mallon wasn't dead. He had to get over him.

"We've got to make them give a damn," a voice hollered from somewhere behind and was met with a wall of approval.

"But how?" Someone else asked.

"They don't want to know."

Anjoa, a beautiful Black trans woman who DJ'd at The New Inn, got to her feet and waved at the crowd to be quiet. Anjoa was a member of the Blyham Pride committee, and when she spoke, people listened. "We are all angry tonight and with good fucking reason. We'll decide in the next few days the best course of action we can take to raise awareness — marches, demonstrations, fundraisers. We'll do everything we can to make the voices of these victims heard and force the police to get justice for them."

Her words were met with applause. Roman and Ashley joined in. He needed to. Whatever action was decided upon, he would be part of it. He'd experienced first-hand the kind of abuse his people were suffering. It was time to fight back.

"But before all that," Anjoa continued, "there's something far more important we need to do. Keep safe. Look out for each other. No one else will do it for us. We need to take care of ourselves. Starting right now, tonight, you need to be vigilant. There are too many bastards out there who want to hurt us. Not all of them are killers, but they'll beat the shit out of you if they get the chance."

Ashley put a reassuring hand on Roman's forearm. "You okay?" he mouthed.

Roman nodded. He didn't want sympathy or to make any of this about him. It was about Cameron, the five other victims and protecting anyone from future danger.

"No more risks," Phil yelled. "No casual hook-ups with sketchy men who won't even give you their name. No going down dark alleys with strangers. No inviting dubious people home. And if you really must do all that, make sure someone sees you. Meet them in a public place first. Get their fucking faces on CCTV. Tell your friends what you're up to. Safe call each other. If you don't want to take someone home, then drag their arses to The Viaduct. You can fuck them there. It's a safe space with plenty of staff and security. You won't be alone."

Phil's words were met with more serious applause. No one laughed or cheered or thought any of it was funny. The world had changed. Their lives had been touched by darkness.

There was a palpable sense of fear among the crowd. So thick, Roman felt like he could touch it. He shared it, too. What had happened to Cameron could easily have happened to him or Ashley or any of their friends.

Everything Anjoa and Phil had said was right.

The danger was real, and it was here, and any one of them could be next.

Chapter Eight

Rising Tensions

The rest of the year came and went. Several of the men who had been associates or lovers of Cameron Taylor were picked up by the cops for questioning. They were all later released without charge. The LGBTQ community accused Blyham Police of a witch hunt. Rather than make legitimate headway into the investigation, it was easier for them to round up other gay guys and haul them in. Tension with law enforcement officers was at an all-time high.

The only good Roman saw to come out of it was a reduction in general hate crimes across the village. A young gay guy had been killed in a hit and run on the waterfront, right in front of The Vermont Hotel, but as it had occurred outside of the LGBTQ sector, no one saw it as being related. The driver had not been found. Blyham Police had finally put more uniforms on patrol and employed a liaison officer to instil some faith. With the patrons of the village no longer such easy targets, the incidents of abuse fell considerably, not that he noticed any change in behaviour. People were scared and afraid to go out alone. Throughout the Christmas and New Year periods, he had never seen the venues so empty. It was safer to stay away or frequent the mainstream city centre bars and clubs.

Only The Viaduct seemed to thrive. With everyone cautious of going home with a potentially deadly strangler, the arches and corridors of The Viaduct were the safest place to get off.

Roman had moderated his own behaviour since that weekend in October and had only had a single hook-up in that whole time. He'd met a guy online, and after a few conversations, they'd got together for coffee before going back to Roman's place for sex. It had been pretty good, and Benito, a local guy of Italian heritage in his early thirties, had been a hottie, but there was no magic. Benito had messaged him afterwards, interested in a second date, and he'd suggested going for a meal that time, but Roman couldn't see the point in stringing him along when he had no intention of taking it further.

Benito had seemed like a nice guy, but Roman was not in the market for a boyfriend.

However, when he did go out, he still kept his eyes open, hoping to see Mallon again, but in two months, there had been no sign of the sexy Frenchman.

In early January, the Pride committee announced a joint meeting to be held at the town hall with representatives from the police.

"We should go," Roman had said when Ashley informed him of the plan.

"What good will it do?"

"It lets them know we're still here and that they need to do a lot more to catch the Blyham-fucking-Strangler."

It had not escaped anyone's attention that the killer had been working to a schedule for a year and half, with a new murder committed every two-to-four months. If he stuck to that timetable, he would claim his next victim sometime between January and March. With a growing sense of urgency, Roman and Ashley set out one Friday evening to attend the event at the town hall.

Roman had to leave work on the dot to get there in time. It wasn't ideal. His employers had warned of a downturn in business and the need to make cuts in the first quarter of the year. Roman had done all he could to show willingness to his bosses — arriving early, staying late and taking short lunch breaks most days. He hadn't left on time in weeks, but tonight was too important for him to miss.

It was a cold evening. In his winter jacket, leather gloves and the woollen scarf his mother had given him for Christmas, he still felt the chill as they walked through the streets. Breath swirled in vapours around his head, and his feet were numb. So far, snow had held off, though with cold this fierce, he felt it couldn't be far away.

It was a relief to step into the warmth of the town hall foyer. A notice in the entrance said the LGBTQ Liaison meeting was being held in a function room on the first floor. It was an old building from the early 1900s. Despite a grand exterior, the inside had suffered from a low budget refit sometime in the last ten years and had the over-lit, plastic appearance of a motorway service station.

"I haven't been here since my cousin got married," Ashley admitted as they climbed the stairs.

"It's an unusual venue for a wedding," Roman said, taking in the characterless modern features.

"All she could afford...cheap and cheerful. They've got a good catering team, and the bar has dirt bargain-basement prices. And I remember sucking off one of the groom's mates in the toilets." He pointed along the corridor when they reached the first floor. "Down there."

Roman laughed. "They should hire you as a tour guide. You could entertain the tourists with your colourful local tales. 'Places I have shagged'."

"Bitch," Ashley tutted. "Anyone would think you weren't the man who has a revolving door on his arse."

"That was last year," he corrected. "A lot has changed since then."

"I'll say it bloody has," Ashley muttered.

The door to the function room was propped open. It was nearly full when they entered, ten minutes before the meeting was due to start.

"Whoa," Roman said. "I didn't expect such a big turn out."

"Me neither. At least it will make the cops take notice."

"The press, too." He pointed out a reporter and two camera operators at the front.

"Good. And I hope this time they report something worthwhile instead of putting out another victim-shaming piece."

They worked their way through the aisles, looking for two seats together, eventually finding them in the middle of the eighth row.

A handsome dark-haired guy in his early thirties waved at Roman from four rows back. He smiled and returned the wave, uncertain who the man was.

Ashley didn't miss the gesture. "Who is that? He's dishy."

"Not sure yet," Roman whispered back. "It will come to me."

Ashley snorted. "Someone who went through the revolving door, I'm sure."

"You could be right." By the time Roman took his seat, his memory snapped into focus. "John," he whispered excitedly. "Or Jack. Something with a J. I met him at The Viaduct last summer. I've seen him around a few times since, but we haven't...you know."

Ashley rolled his eyes. "You and that place. I wouldn't set foot in there if you paid me...even now." He turned his head, seeming to scan to room, but angling for a closer look at the hottie. "Actually, he's quite nice. I wouldn't have thought someone as wholesome-looking as him would go to that dump."

"Looks are deceiving," Roman said as his memory became more focused. "I thought I'd bagged a big hunky Daddy to...you know."

"Smash your back doors in. And what? Don't tell me. He was an even bigger bottom than you are."

Roman nodded, suppressing a laugh. "Stop staring at him."

"I bet that was something to behold. Two greedy bottoms arguing over who was gonna get it. What did you do? Just squash your buttholes together for a bit of friction?"

Roman flushed and gently elbowed him. "Shush. This is not the place."

Ashley scoffed. "Thought so. Aren't I always right about these things?"

"Don't be so dismissive. Booty to booty...it's a thing."

"For desperate bottoms who make the mistake of hooking up together."

They each put a fist in their mouths to contain their laughter. It was totally inappropriate, but after all the bad news and anxiety, it was a relief to make fun of something so daft.

Roman composed himself. This was serious business, and they should show respect. The meeting was called to order at exactly six o'clock. He recognised most of the members of the committee at the front of the room. Anjoa, the DJ from The New Inn took a seat on the stage next to Phil. Phil had been the most pro-active of all the bar managers in the village. He'd already held three charity events in memory of the victims. He'd arranged vigils and had set up a neighbourhood watch programme of volunteers to patrol the streets every weekend, looking for people who might be vulnerable from drug or alcohol use and helping them to get home safely. He also provided free personal alarms for anyone who came to the bar and asked for one. Phil had been a major driving force in the community over the dark, winter months...a true local hero.

A handful of others took to the stage. Police officers, Roman assumed, then he caught his breath as someone he did recognise sat down at the side.

"What's the matter?" Ashley whispered.

"That guy in the blue jacket. I know him." Benito...the handsome Italian who had wanted to take him out last autumn. He looked good, damned good, in a navy suit and open-necked shirt. The colours complemented his dark, Mediterranean skin tone.

"Is there anyone here you haven't shagged?" Ashley muttered from the side of his mouth.

"I didn't know he was a cop." He struggled to recall what Benito had told him about himself, but Roman would definitely have remembered if he'd said he was a police officer. Like many people he knew, Roman had a distrust of the police. They had done little to support the community, and through most of their investigations, they had displayed a clear policy of victim blaming. Homophobia ran deep through the Blyham Police Force, and Roman doubted they would have much to say this evening that would change his mind.

* * * *

"Waste of fucking time," Ashley said.

They were in a corner table at Julie's following the meeting, two long and unproductive hours that had done more to rattle the attendees than reassure them.

"I think they listened to some of our concerns," Anjoa said. The tone of her voice lacked the conviction of her words.

"I bet they were taking note of everyone who was there, wondering whether they could add us to their suspect list," Ashley said. "It's obvious that they've got fuck all else to go on."

"I don't think it was quite that bad," Phil said, trying to placate him.

"It was," Ashley said vehemently. "It was a box-ticking PR exercise so they can pretend they are listening."

Roman didn't share Ashley's anger at the lack of progress made by Blyham Police, but he had come away from the meeting feeling dejected and in a low mood. Why had the discovery of Benito's work bothered him so much? He knew what Ashley would say—*because you've been sleeping with the enemy.* He couldn't deny he did feel that way. And why had Benito kept quiet about his career? Had he been snooping? Gong undercover and pretending to be one of them? Overstepping professional boundaries to shag the suspects?

Benito hadn't spoken once during the whole meeting, which made Roman wonder what he'd been doing there at all. Unless it was what Ashley suspected and he was there to keep an eye on the crowd and look for suspects. But if that was the case, why would he take to the stage at all?

Why do you even care? He was an okay fuck you weren't even interested in. What's the big deal now?

Something about his presence had angered Roman but he didn't know what for sure. He wouldn't have felt anywhere near as strongly had Benito been sitting in the audience with the rest of them.

"So, what happens now?" he asked. "If this guy is still around, the timer is running down on when he's going to strike again. What are we going to do?"

"Keep safe," Phil said, fidgeting with his cigarette lighter. "Remain vigilant and look out for one another. We owe it to ourselves to make it as difficult as possible for this lunatic to claim another victim."

Ashley nodded agreement.

"It's going to take a lot more than that," Anjoa said. "Those cops said they were going to put more officers on the beat. That's fine for dealing with general hate crime, but this guy, this strangler, he's not choosing his victims from the street. He's killing them in their own homes. We need to educate people every single day about the risk they are in."

"Agreed," Phil said. "But it's hard to see how we could be doing any more than we are."

"We *have* to," she insisted.

Roman supressed a sigh. This was getting frustrating. They were going around in circles and achieving nothing. He didn't know what the answer was either but was sick of the endless debate. Seeing Bentio had put him a foul mood he found difficult to shake. "I'm going for a piss," he said, sliding out from behind the table.

It was almost nine, and the front of the bar was at a third of capacity. The DJ was in her booth paying the usual mixed of chart and camp hits, but like all the bars in Blyham, Julie's had taken a hit, Roman doubted there was much future for any of the bars if the strangler wasn't caught soon.

The thought only depressed him further.

Julie's was an old pub, and the bathrooms hadn't had a refit since the 1980s. The place was bare and functional with no heating. Roman's breath rose in vapours around his face as soon as he stepped inside. He shivered as he unfastened his fly and pissed into the urinal. More steam rose from the gutter.

He needed to shake himself out of this mood. He could barely afford to come out tonight. His earnings were stretched so thinly that disposable income was a thing of the past. If he was going to go broke over a few drinks, he'd make damn sure he enjoyed them.

He washed his hands under the freezing cold tap and tried to warm them beneath the drier.

Suddenly someone seized him from behind.

He gasped and panicked as strong arms closed around his trunk and squeezed him tight. He struggled to breathe.

Fuck. Not here. Not like this.

Roman was about to scream for help when he felt hot breath on the back of his ear and a heavily accented voice said, "I've missed that sexy ass."

Now he gasped in pleasure.

Mallon loosened his grip and spun him around.

Before Roman could answer, Mallon forced his mouth on top of his. He thrust his tongue inside, and Roman did not resist.

Chapter Nine

Reunited

"When did you return?" Roman gasped when Mallon released him after a long, lingering kiss.

Mallon's hands roamed all across Roman's torso, feeling him up beneath his clothes.

"About three weeks ago," he said, pulling Roman's hips against his own, where the bulk of his hard cock could not be mistaken.

"Oh." Roman tried to hide his disappointment. They hadn't exchanged numbers, so how could Mallon have gotten in touch?

Mallon gave him a dimpled smile, reading his displeasure. "Relax. I've been busy." He gripped Roman's backside in two hands, squeezing his flesh. "This is the first time I've been out since getting back. I hoped you would be here."

Roman brightened, leaning into Mallon's taut body, relishing how his hands kneaded his arse. "You did?" It could have been a line, but he was happy to fall for it. Roman was already thinking with his hole instead of his head.

Mallon looked hot as hell in a thick, winter jacket. He wouldn't have thought the same on most other guys, but Mallon could pull off anything. Roman had had no interest in Benito, or any other man since that night in October, and a few seconds with Mallon had him feeling hot and eager. No one else compared. Roman jammed his lips against Mallon's, hungry for another kiss. He shoved his tongue into his mouth, savouring the taste and scent he remembered so well. He planted his hands on the French man's butt, pulling their hips even tighter together.

"You've missed me," Mallon said, moving his lips against Roman's.

Roman nodded, planting kisses along the side of his mouth.

"Have you missed me, or is your ass just hungry for a good fuck?"

Roman's cock swelled to another dimension. *How is it possible to be so turned on?*

"I missed everything," he whispered.

Mallon loosened his hold and gave his butt a playful slap. "Then why are we wasting time in this freezing cold piss hole. Let's go."

Roman's felt his pulse racing all through his body. He hadn't appreciated how horny he was until Mallon appeared. He'd triggered something inside him that had been switched off since autumn. *Lust.*

"Let me get my jacket and tell my friends I'm leaving."

"I'll wait at the door."

Roman raced to the table. The conversation was still going round in circles, debating what they could do next.

"Sorry, guys, but I have to leave it here." He pulled on his jacket and gathered his scarf and gloves.

"Where are you going?" Ashley fixed him with sharp, narrow eyes.

"I just ran into someone I know. We're going to…catch up."

"You met someone in the toilet?" Ashley arched a judgemental eyebrow. "Who?"

"You don't know him." Roman withered under Ashley's penetrating stare. "Okay," he yielded. "It's someone I met a few months ago. I told you about him. The Frenchman. Mallon."

"Are you fucking serious?" Anjoa said. "After everything we've been talking about, you're going off for a random hook-up. Jesus. Will you horny guys ever stop thinking with your dicks?"

"It's not like that," he argued. "Look… This isn't some weirdo. I know him. I trust him."

Ashley shook his head. "Unbelievable. We're fighting a losing battle here. How can we expect guys to stay safe when just one sniff of cock is all it takes to make them run headlong into danger?"

"Come on. You're being a drama queen. I'm not taking any risks. I already know Mallon. Besides, he's just been in here, so he's going to be all over the CCTV footage. If I don't come home tomorrow, you'll know who to look for."

"Don't make light of this," Phil said, fixing him with a serious stare. "It's not a thing to joke about. Take every precaution. Text Ashley later to let him know where you are. And share you location if you go back to this man's place instead of home."

"All right, I will. But this is the guy who saved me from a group attack last October. I don't think he's about to turn on me now."

"Just do it to keep us from worrying, okay?"

He raised his hands in submission. "I will. But you're wrong about this man. I'll be in no danger with him."

As Roman walked away Ashley called after him, "I hope you're fucking right, 'cause you might not wake up tomorrow otherwise."

There was no point in arguing. They would keep him here all night if he allowed them to.

Mallon waited at the front door, smoking a cigarette. He turned his head slightly and gave an eyebrow twitch of acknowledgement. Roman shivered and fastened his coat, wrapping the scarf around his neck. The temperature had plummeted in the time he'd been inside.

"Shall we get an Uber?" Roman asked.

"We can walk to the taxi rank," Mallon answered. "It's not far, and it's not late. You'll be safe with me."

Roman fell into step beside him, and they headed up Salvin Road. It didn't escape his notice that he'd been walking this exact route, from Julie's to the taxi rank, when they'd first encountered each other.

Two uniformed police officers passed by on the other side of the road. If they had bothered with more regular patrols last year, Roman and Mallon might never have met.

"A lot of cops about," Mallon observed. "Did you report what happened to you last year?"

"I did."

"Did they ever catch the men who attacked you?"

"No. I don't think they ever looked."

"Typical." He paused to stub out his cigarette in a waste bin. He shoved his hands in his pockets and kept walking. "That's the third group of cops I've seen all night. What's the emergency?"

The cold bit into Roman's ears, and he pulled his hat lower to cover the tips. "Don't you know about the murders?"

Mallon turned to look at him. "I remember hearing something last time I was here. Haven't they caught who was responsible for that, either?"

It seemed incredible that Mallon knew so little about what was going on when it was such a hot topic for everyone he knew. Then he remembered two major factors. Mallon didn't live here. He was a visiting businessman. And even more relevant, the mainstream coverage of the killings had been minimal. A couple of the national newspapers had run with the story after the two most recent murders, but they had revelled in the salacious details of the victim's lifestyle, coming to blame them and their behaviour for their deaths. There had been nothing major since. He wondered if anyone outside of Blyham's LGBTQ community were even aware of the troubles. From what Mallon had just said, it sounded unlikely.

Roman filled him in on the Blyham Strangler.

"Five men dead so far, and the police are no closer to catching the killer. Do you remember Cameron? The guy you were with in The Viaduct on the night you met me?"

"Not really."

"Oh."

"Should I?"

"I suppose not. Only he's one of the victims."

Mallon swore in French and shook his head. "Five dead *queer* men is not the same, is it? If someone murdered five straight guys from a football team, or golf buddies, they would throw every resource into catching their killer. No?" There was a bitter tone to his voice.

"It feels that way." Roman glanced over his shoulder. The two police officers were out of sight. It was hard not to feel anger towards them. How long would they continue to patrol the streets, anyway? If no one fell victim to the killer in the next few weeks, they would drift back to their important duties. If the Blyham Strangler wanted to remain at large, all they had to do was wait. The cops would disappear soon enough.

Roman was freezing by the time they reached they taxi rank. The cold had seeped through his boots and chilled him from the toes upwards. He was relieved to see three cars at the kerb and no one waiting for them. They jumped into the back and Mallon gave the driver an address. No discussion over where they were going, Roman's place or his. Roman didn't mind. It would make everything a lot simpler if Mallon didn't have to face a pissy Ashley in the morning.

He slid close to Mallon on the back seat, pressing their legs together and shivering.

"Soon you'll be warm," Mallon assured him, sliding his gloved hand up Roman's thigh, letting it rest against his crotch.

Despite the cold, Roman's cock stiffened. This was not where he had expected his evening to end, but he was thrilled at the development.

The taxi drove along the waterfront, passing by The Vermont Hotel without stopping.

"We're not getting out. Are you staying somewhere else now."

Mallon leaned closer, his breath hot against Roman's face. "You'll see." He gave his thigh a squeeze.

The taxi came to a stop in front of a new building that been completed approximately two years ago. It was modern and minimal and didn't really suit the architecture of the waterfront. One of the those building Roman saw most days without ever paying any interest. They got out, and Mallon paid the driver. As Roman looked up at the building, which had to be at least twelve storeys high, he realised it was a fancy apartment block with balconies looking out onto the river.

"You're staying here?" he asked as Mallon came up beside him and tapped his arse, encouraging him to the main entrance.

"It's cheaper than the hotel now that I have to be here for more than a few nights. Alas, no penthouse apartment, but it's sufficient for the time I spend here."

He used a key card to enter the secure door, leading into to a fancy foyer. It was still one-hundred-percent nicer than any of the hotels Roman had stayed in, except for his night with Mallon at the Vermont. He moved towards the elevator.

"We can take the stairs," Mallon said with a smile, guiding him to a passageway on the left. "I told you, no penthouse. My apartment is on the first floor."

Mallon's word caused Roman to lower his expectations, which was a mistake. Mallon's apartment was much bigger and swankier than the room he'd had at the hotel. The main living area was open plan with a high-end kitchen area on one side, all modern white units and black granite surfaces, while there were brown leather sofas and a huge mahogany coffee table in front of the floor-to-ceiling windows that opened onto a balcony terrace.

"Fuck," Roman gasped. "What the hell is the penthouse like, if this is what you get on the first floor?"

"I don't know," Mallon said, taking off his jacket and hanging it over a chair at the breakfast bar. "I haven't been up to see. But this will do for now."

"What do you do to be able to afford all this?" The words were out before Roman could stop them. He knew it was rude, but he couldn't help it. He wanted to know.

"I'm a project manager. Ever heard of AgeronBus?"

"No. Never."

"You will. It's a French engineering and manufacturing company. We are expanding with a new factory right here on an estate outside of the city. A lot of jobs and investments will come on the back of it. It will soon be a very big deal in Blyham" Mallon moved behind the kitchen counter and opened the fridge. "Vodka for you, right?"

"Great," Roman said, pulling off his gloves and scarf and attempting to brush his hair into some kind of style. He took off his coat and hung it over the back of a chair beside Mallon's. He knew he should text Ashley and let him know where he was, especially after the fuss they had made, but he didn't want to ruin the mood. He would do it in a while.

There was nothing personal about the apartment — no family photos or books, not even a stray magazine lying around. It was just as anonymous as the hotel room where he'd stayed before.

"How long are you here for?" he asked.

"The lease is for six months," Mallon said, pouring a generous splash of whisky. "It can be extended if needs be. I won't be here all that time, though. I'll be travelling back and forth between Blyham and Lyon."

"Wow. That's quite a lifestyle." Roman was quietly pleased to hear Mallon would be around longer than expected. If he were lucky, this didn't have to be such a casual arrangement.

Mallon came from behind the counter, moving with languid sensuality. His jeans hugged his long limbs, bulging at the crotch. He wore a navy-and-white striped sweater, which hung beautifully on his wide shoulders and toned chest. He handed Roman his drink and raised his own glass.

"Cheers."

"Cheers." Roman gazed into his pale grey eyes as they clinked glasses. *Shit. He's even sexier than I remembered.* He sipped the drink, which was a lot more vodka than mixer. "Whoa. That's strong."

"It's good, though. None of that cheap shit you drink in the bars."

Roman laughed. "Cheap shit is all I can afford. You'll get used to it, if you stick around long enough."

"I'll never get used to such inferior muck," Mallon grimaced. He sat on the sofa and crossed an ankle over his knee, a pose Roman remembered so well. "I've missed your ass."

Roman laughed uncertainly. Mallon's directness could be beguiling. "Don't you get all the arse you want in France?"

Mallon cocked an eyebrow and his dimples deepened. "Not like yours. Take off your pants. Show me what I missed."

Roman glanced at the huge windows. He could see across the river and lights in the buildings on the other side. "They'll see."

"They can't see. It's too far. Stop delaying. Ass now, please."

His boldness was impossible to resist. Roman put his drink on the coffee table and sat to remove his winter walking boots. He was aware of Mallon watching every move as he stood again and undid his belt and fly. His shoved his jeans to his ankles and stepped out of them. When he'd come out this evening, he'd had no plans to go home with anyone, and the underpants he'd chosen were functional rather than sexy—a pair of thick, navy trunks that came midway down his thigh.

"I didn't expect to meet you tonight," he said, tugging at the heavy cotton.

Mallon sipped his whisky and licked his lips. "You know what to do. Turn around and take them off."

Since the last time, Roman had fantasied about this moment. He knew what Mallon liked and how to give to him. So what if his pants had been chosen for the cold weather… He was more than willing to deliver. He slipped his boxer-briefs down slowly, revealing his buttocks an inch at a time…lower, lower, until his full arse was on display. He raised the hem of his sweater to present an unhindered view, transferring weight from one leg to the other to make his arse swell. Then he shucked his trunks all the way down and off. He straightened, planted both hands on his cheeks and spread himself slowly, revealing his hole.

Mallon made a noise from deep in his throat, then he was off the sofa and on his knees right behind him. Mallon gripped Roman's waist, and he buried his face in his crack. Roman gasped and rose onto his toes as Mallon's tongue went straight for his hole, swirling around the rim with deliciously wet strokes.

"Oh my God." Roman's entire body shuddered. He'd forgotten just how great Mallon was at eating arse.

The Frenchman devoured him like a feast— slurping, probing, tasting, inhaling, enjoying his arse to the full. Roman touched his own cock, which was as hard as steel, leaking pre-cum down the length of the shaft to his balls.

Mallon pulled him to the floor, then rolled him onto his side. "I need to be inside you." He fumbled with his clothes, shoving his jeans and underwear to his knees. He produced a small sachet of lube from somewhere and tore into it with his teeth. Wet, sticky fingers slivered into Roman's crack, going straight for his hole and pushing inside. Roman arched his back and gave his body up.

Mallon moved tight behind him. Roman raised his right leg and held the back of his thigh to give easy access. He shivered when the wet tip of Mallon's cock grazed his hole, then the wonderful pressure as Mallon leaned his hips into him and his cock spread his opening. Roman took a deep breath as Mallon stretched him and held it until he pushed through his sphincter. Mallon's cock slipped all the way inside.

"Oh God," Roman cried, resting his head on his outstretched arm, relishing the sensations of being totally impaled.

Mallon's mouth fastened on the back of Roman's neck, biting gently as he thrust. He snarled and gripped him tighter. Nothing compared to the feeling of being so thoroughly filled by a huge dick. They groaned in unison. Mallon bucked and shoved, utterly consumed by passion. Roman willed his body to open farther and pushed back against him. Three months of unspent desire for each other made Roman dizzy. They rutted and shoved like animals. Mallon came quickly. With a roar he buried his cock to the hilt and filled Roman with his load. The pulse of Mallon's cock inside was all Roman needed to trigger his own release, and he unloaded all over the bland cream carpet.

"Oh, man," Mallon groaned, leaving his cock inside when he was done. "I needed this ass even more than I anticipated."

Chapter Ten

Breakfast and After

"I have no food in the kitchen," Mallon said, coming out of the bathroom with a white towel wrapped around his waist. His bronzed skin glistened, still wet from the shower. He had the most remarkable suntan, considering it was winter. Roman didn't know a lot about the climate in France, but wherever it was that Mallon lived, it seemed unlikely he could have acquired it naturally at this time of year. "Get dressed, and I'll take you for breakfast."

Roman stretched languorously, arching his back and pushing his limbs into the corners of the bed. He yawned and murmured his appreciation. "Can I shower first?"

"Quickly," Mallon said, whipping the towel from his waist to dry his hair. There was a perfect stretch of white skin below his waist to the top of his thighs, before the suntan started again.

Roman rolled off the bed and strode naked into the bathroom. He hadn't slept much. Just like their first time, the night had been filled with passion and fucking, but he felt gloriously refreshed and awake this morning. Five minutes later, he was showered, dried and searching for his clothes, which were scattered around the living room. Mallon was already dressed, looking hotter than hell in faded jeans, a pale blue shirt, a dark grey, V-neck cashmere sweater and dark brown brogues. He pulled on his winter jacket with the fur trim.

"Very stylish," Roman remarked as they left the apartment, feeling underdressed in last night's clothes.

The waterfront of Blyham was a mix of old and new venues, traditional menus and cutting-edge cuisine, chain pubs and cafes, independent eateries and sandwich bars. Roman rarely paid much attention to this area of the city, but as he walked along the river side, inhaling the frosty air with Mallon beside him, he developed an all-new appreciation for the place.

It was no surprise when Mallon passed the well-known chain of coffee shops to lead him into an independent bistro called The Grind. Roman had heard good word of mouth about it from people at work, but this was his first visit. It was smaller than he expected, with around ten tables and a couple of soft-seat areas. The café was around eighty-percent full already. Mallon slipped into a seat at an empty table near the window and picked up the menu. *He acts like he owns the place. He probably could if he wanted to*, Roman thought. He obviously earned a huge salary to support his lifestyle.

"What's good?" Roman asked. He was buzzing inside and struggling to play it cool. How amazing was this? Having a late breakfast with the hot older man he's been obsessing over for months? It was quite unreal and yet everything he wanted.

Mallon shrugged. "It's all good. It depends on what you like."

A young server with multicoloured dreadlocks came to the table. "Can I get you anything to drink first?" she asked brightly.

Mallon ordered orange juice and black coffee. When Roman asked for a latte, he caught the expression of disapproval that passed over Mallon's face. *Tough.* He wasn't about to suffer bitter black coffee to impress the Frenchman, no matter how sexy he was.

"Is this where you have all your meals?" Roman asked.

"Mostly breakfast," Mallon answered, looking at him over the menu. "But they do take away, too. I've also gotten food after work from here."

"Do you ever cook? Or is that fancy kitchen just for show?"

"I like good food, fine food…better than I can cook for myself. There's not much to choose from in your city, so I stick to the same few places I like."

"Fine food. Fine whisky. What other fine things do you like?"

Mallon lowered the menu, his mouth twisted in a lop-sided grin. "Fine wine." He reduced his voice to a whisper. "Fine ass."

Heat rose to Roman's face. "You're a man who knows what he likes."

"Always."

When the server returned with their drinks, Mallon ordered a potato and cheese rosti with streaky bacon, Portobello mushrooms and a fried egg. After changing his mind three times, Roman settled on sourdough toast topped with sauteed mushroom, Emmental cheese and a poached egg.

"This place is quite something," he said. "It's a big step up from the greasy café I sometimes visit on my way to work. Bacon or sausage butties are as extravagant as it gets."

Mallon grimaced, making Roman smile. He was clearly a snob when it came to food and drink, but it made a nice change to the humdrum tastes of the men he usually met.

He added a heaped spoon of brown sugar to his latte. "You said you're a project manager. What is it you manage?"

"It will be boring to you."

"No, I'm interested…seriously, especially if you are bringing new jobs to Blyham. I could be on the market for one of those sooner than I'd like."

"I'm overseeing the construction and start-up of the new factory. Once it's up and running, we have contracts to produce railway carriages and coaches. Big investments. Big opportunities for Blyham."

"It sounds like it."

"And what is it you do?" Mallon asked.

"Now this will bore you because it bores me. I work on the customer service helpline for a domestic appliance firm, helping people when their washing machines and ovens go wrong. Boring, right? This is the first Saturday I've had off in weeks, too."

"Why don't you find something else if you hate it so much?"

"If it was that easy, I would. I have a degree in economics, and I worked for two years as a chartered accountant until the firm went bust. I've struggled to find another job in the same field, which is why I'm answering calls about faulty appliances. I don't know how long I can manage that for. The money is rubbish, as well as the job being boring. There's a threat of redundancies on the horizon, too. If the job situation doesn't improve in the next six months, I might have to move back home."

"And where is home?"

"A small town up the coast. It's called Nyemouth. It's a nice place, pretty, but unless you're in the fishing or the hospitality sector, the job prospects there are even worse than here. At least I won't have rent to pay, but moving in with my parents in my mid-twenties is not how I thought my life would pan out."

"Fishermen and hotel owners need accountants, too. There are always opportunities if you look for them."

"Not in Nyemouth. You wouldn't say that if you knew the place." Roman had spent the entirety of his teenage years wanting to escape the small-town life he'd been brought up with. Since moving to Blyham for university, he had not gone back for anything other than birthday and Christmas visits. His life would be a failure if he had to return there now.

Mallon devoured his breakfast with unbridled hunger, picking up the napkin to wipe his lips once the plate was cleared. He was clearly a man of intense appetites. Roman took his time, savouring the food. This was a real treat, and he didn't want to waste it. Mallon signalled for another coffee.

"You're enjoying it?" he asked.

Roman nodded, still chewing.

"The first few times I came to this city, I found the food unbearable," Mallon said, pulling a face. "All the same fast food and chain shops you find anywhere in the world... It took a while to discover the better places. There aren't too many, but they are here, if you know where to look."

"I've lived in Blyham for years, and this is the first time I've been in here. I'm happy with a burger, a pizza or a big bowl of pasta. I don't go for fancy meals."

Mallon's lips twitched downwards. Roman suppressed a smile and continued eating. Was their attraction based on nothing but sex? They appeared to have little else in common. Despite that, Roman wanted to get to know him and learn more about the things Mallon liked.

"What else do you do here?" he asked. "When you're not working or having fancy dinners?"

"Not a lot. I go into the office early and return late most days. Some evenings I might have dinner with colleagues or clients."

"Which is just more work. What do you do to relax?"

"I fuck you," he said, his grey eyes sparkling. "I find that very relaxing."

"We've only spent two nights together, in what…three, four months?"

"I told you, I don't have a lot of free time. When I do, I return to France."

Does that mean I'm not one in a long line of casual fuckboys? Or is he just spinning me a line that he thinks I want to hear?

"It sounds lonely…and stressful, all those hours at work with no serious down time."

Mallon shrugged. "I haven't found much in Blyham to interest me."

"It doesn't sound like you've made any effort. There's a lot more to the city than you would think. Don't dismiss it too quickly."

"Okay. What do you suggest? What do you do when you're not at work — or fucking strange men?"

"Do you like football?"

Mallon grimaced harder than ever.

Roman laughed. "I'll take that as a no. I follow Blyham FC, but I can't afford the tickets much. I only make it to occasional games. But I like to watch the matches in the pub if they are on TV."

"You are not convincing me. Is that all this city has? A football team?"

"No. There are lots of museums and art galleries. There's the castle further along the river, cinema's, exhibitions. There's a theatre and a concert hall. In the summer, they have a lot of open-air concerts in the grounds of the castle. You can hear all kinds of live music — pop, rock, dance, opera. There are churches and a large cathedral, markets and street food. There's a lot to Blyham, but you just haven't discovered it yet."

"So it would seem," he said, sitting back and watching Roman with keen eyes. "Maybe I have underestimated this place."

"A lot of people do."

"And maybe you can show me some of these things."

Roman put down his knife and fork as Mallon's words sent a rush right through him. "I'd love to, whenever you want."

After breakfast, Mallon suggested a walk farther along to the waterfront to help the food digest. It was still freezing outside, but Roman would agree to anything just to spend more time with him. Mallon lit a cigarette as he walked. Smoking had always been a turn off, but like most things with Mallon, he didn't even mind that.

He pointed out a modern building on the other side of the river, the entire exterior of which was mirrored glass. "That's Blyham Concert Hall. It's only been open around three years, but it's a great venue. They have all kinds of music playing. You should check out what is on. There's bound to be something that suits you, and it's so close to your apartment. They have a huge main hall and a smaller studio for more intimate concerts."

"Maybe. I'm not a fan of crowded places, so I tend to avoid concerts and theatres."

"There's a coffee shop in there and a small art gallery, so it's still worth your while to check it out."

"All right. You win. I'll have a look someday. You have convinced me that there is more to your city than I first assumed."

It was late morning, and the usual gaggle of Saturday stag and hen parties started to arrive and fill up the bars. Despite the January cold, they came out in their skimpy dresses and loose shirts to brave the waterfront.

Roman indicated a path to their right. "We can cut up there and walk along the parallel street back to your apartment. It avoids the worst of the party gangs. They get rowdy quickly at the weekend. Most of them will have been drinking already."

When they were off the main street, Mallon put out his cigarette and moved closer, putting an arm around Roman's waist. Roman twitched with excitement. His cock was on a hair-trigger. The slightest touch or gesture from Mallon was all it took to get a stiff rise.

"I have a hard on," Mallon announced.

"That makes two of us."

"I've had one for the last half hour." Mallon leaned over and nuzzled Roman's cold ear.

"We don't have far to go."

Mallon pulled him even closer. "I can't wait."

They approached a narrow alley leading between a hotel and a restaurant. Mallon drove him down the gap.

"What are you doing?" Roman looked around in both directions. At least they were alone.

"I want you now." Mallon said, shuffling behind a large waste bin. He put his back against the wall and unbuckled his belt.

"Here?" Roman gasped. "It's freezing." The cobbles beneath his feet were still coated in frost that had yet to thaw.

Mallon put a hand on his shoulder and urged him down. He'd already unfastened his fly. He yanked his jeans open and released his hard cock from his underpants. "There you go," he said, pressing a thumb against the base of his cock and pointing it towards Roman. "Suck me."

Roman looked around again. He could hear music and voices drifting from the river side and had no idea if any of the windows above them looked directly down. He didn't care. He couldn't say no to Mallon or resist this beautiful dick. With a final check, he took off his hat and stuffed it into his pocket. He slid his tongue along the underside of the head and opened his mouth wide, taking his dick to the back of his throat. Mallon's cock was good and sticky with pre-cum, and Roman realised he hadn't been lying about being hard for so long. Mallon groaned and wrapped his hands around Roman's head.

Roman steadied himself against his thighs and worked him with only his mouth, taking him deep enough to gag before withdrawing all the way to the tip. Mallon's dick throbbed each time he deep-throated.

He jerked his hips forward, gently leaning in to fuck Roman's face.

Roman had to hurry him along. They couldn't afford to be caught in the act. He bobbed his head faster, summoning more spit and creating suction. Mallon's fingers raked through his hair and twisted. He gasped. "Oh, that's it. Yes. Going to come."

Roman kept him in his mouth, on the soft cushion of his tongue and thrilled as Mallon flooded him with his hot, salty seed. He swallowed, amazed at the volume. Mallon had come at least four times last night and still managed to produce a massive load this morning. He was a sexual superbeing.

He laughed, leaning against the wall with his jeans undone, his cock still hard, pointing straight out. "That was intense. I prefer to come in an ass, but you have a very talented mouth."

Roman rose to his feet, swallowing, and checked to make sure they were still alone.

"Want me to suck you?" Mallon asked.

"I'd rather not get arrested. I think we've pushed our luck far enough."

Mallon shoved his cock back into his pants. "If you say so. Let's got back to the apartment. I'm going to eat your ass until you beg me to stop."

Roman had no objection to that plan.

Chapter Eleven

Bad News

On Tuesday night, two weeks later, Roman remained at work for an hour of unpaid overtime. It had become a regular event, three or four times a week, as the workers in the help centre fought to avoid the redundancy axe. Roman questioned whether his loyalty was valued by his employer beyond the voluntary labour. The managers had even come to expect it and looked disapprovingly on anyone who packed up and left at the legitimate end of their shift.

It was wrong, but he couldn't do anything to sabotage his work record, not unless he wanted to give up on city life and move in with his parents. He'd applied for fifteen jobs in the last month alone and hadn't obtained a single interview. The employment market was dead.

The cold spell continued. There had been a light layer of snow the previous evening, which had failed to thaw in the sub-zero temperature of the day. Roman fastened his coat to the neck and pulled on his hat and gloves before stepping out through the front door of the office. The air caught the back of his nose and throat. *Damn*, he thought, *it's getting even colder*.

Not cold enough for him to pay for a taxi or even a bus fare home. That was an extravagance he could not afford. He'd prepared that morning by wearing his walking boots and thick socks and set off on the north side of the river for the long walk, with his earbuds in and a podcast for company.

On the other bank, about half a mile down the river, he could see the tall outline of Mallon's building. Too far to determine whether the lights were on in his apartment, but Roman doubted it. From what Mallon had told him, he worked long hours and was rarely home before eight most nights, often later. He might have a highly paid, high-flying job, but he certainly put in a lot of hours. They'd gotten together a few times in the last week, but Mallon had been no more forthcoming with details of his life.

Roman increased his pace. It was not the kind of night to dawdle on the way home. He was starving and looking forward to the leftover pasta he'd stored in the fridge. Food, a couple of hours in front of some trash TV and an early night was just what he needed – a perfect Tuesday evening at home.

He was passing through the town centre when a man walking the other way changed course and approached.

"Hi," the man said, stepping in front of him.

Roman removed the earbuds. There was something familiar about him, though he couldn't quite place him in his winter coat and scarf. He sported a nasty-looking black eye, and there were marks across his nose and cheek.

"I saw you at the meeting the other Friday," the man said. "But you left before I had a chance to talk to you."

Roman looked closer. Blond hair, good-looking. A slight Birmingham accent. *Of course.* One of his many hook-ups from last year. He scrambled through his memory to find a name.

"Will," the man said, spotting his confusion.

Roman blushed. "Sorry. It took me a minute to recognise you." *Only half a lie.* "I don't think I actually saw you at the meeting."

"It was busy, right? I think everyone was surprised by the turn-out."

"Absolutely." Up close, he could see that Will had taken a hell of a beating. "Can I ask you what happened?" He pointed at his battered face. "That looks worrying."

Will raised a hand to his injured eye and gave a shy laugh. "I'm sure you can guess. I ran into the wrong people on my way home on Sunday night. Pretty standard for Blyham these days, don't you think?"

"Oh my God. No. Shit. I'm so sorry. Are you all right?"

"It looks worse than it is. Bruising. I think my pride is more hurt than my face."

"Even still. How did it happen? Where were the police? They were crawling about every street when I was out on Friday."

Will shoved both hands in his pockets and hopped from side to side, as though trying to keep warm. "They jumped me on my way home. I was outside the patrol zone when it happened. Three guys in a car pulled alongside me then got out and started harassing me. After they'd had enough of that, the punches started to fly."

"Shit. That's exactly what happened to me in October." Roman gave him a potted version of his own experience. It was only as he told it that he remembered, he'd actually been in pursuit of Will on the night the thugs had struck. After missing out on Mallon in The Viaduct, he'd spotted Will in Julie's and had tried to follow him for a hook-up. He couldn't decide if he had a terrible memory, or Mallon had come along and made all other men irrelevant. "It sounds like it was probably the same gang. What did they look like?"

Will took a deep breath that hissed through his teeth. "I can't really say, to be honest. My head was all over, trying to find a way to escape, so I didn't take much notice. One of them was big...huge. You know, all jacked up on steroids. Built like a tank. I'm pretty solid, but this guy was huge in comparison. The other two were unremarkable, not as muscled."

"Ginger? Did one of them have ginger hair?"

"It was dark, but one of them was fair, all right. He could have been ginger."

"It sounds like the same bastards. I'm sure of it. Damn. So, they are still out there getting away with this shit. Did you report it to the police?"

Will pulled a face. "What would be the point? The pigs aren't even interested in these random assaults. They only care about catching the Strangler. What would they do? File a report and give me an incident number, at best. It's not worth the aggravation. It would only piss me off having to talk to them."

Roman wanted to tell Will he was wrong, that reporting each crime was in everyone's interest, but he couldn't argue with his way of thinking. He'd thought the same way himself not so long ago. "Next time you are passing Julie's, call in and ask for some anti-attack spray and a personal alarm. They are giving them out for free while all this is going on."

"Isn't it illegal to carry pepper spray?"

"It's not pepper spray. It's a legal self-defence spray. I don't think it does much other than cause a horrible smell, but the chances are the dicks who attacked you won't know that. It stays on their skin and clothes for days afterwards, so it makes them easier to identify."

Will did not look convinced. "I think I'll just play it safe and avoid the village until all this is sorted."

Roman nodded understandingly. "Fair enough. Though there might not be much of a village left soon. The bars have been crippled by the lack of business. Some are talking about closing at the start of the week. It's not worth their while to open until Thursday."

"That's a real shame. But I'm not sure I have the drive to go back right now."

The cold really started to bite as they stood talking. It seeped through the thick soles of Roman's boots and gnawed at his toes. He stomped his feet. "I need to get moving. It's the wrong night to be out. I'm sorry to hear what happened to you, and I hope I do see you out sometime." He smiled and stepped aside, ready to move on.

"Why don't we go somewhere to warm up?" Will said, giving him a hopeful grin. "There's a coffee shop right over there, and they're still serving."

"Oh. I really need to get home," Roman said, remembering their hook-up from last year. Will seemed like a nice guy but there was no chemistry between them, just a random shag who was best left at that. "I'm late already," he lied. "I stayed behind at work tonight." At least that part was true.

Will's smiled wavered. "Okay, no problem. Cool." He shuffled uncomfortably. "Would you…er, like to meet up another time? I thought we had a nice connection, Roman. I'd like to get to know you a bit more."

Roman withered. How could he have such a different memory of their encounter? "I'm kind of seeing someone now," he said.

"Oh. Sorry, I didn't know. You've only been with your friends whenever I've seen you around."

Shit. Our random shag really did mean a lot more to him. Roman struggled to remember seeing much of Will at all since they had their fleeting moment. "It's early days," he said. "He's not into going out on the scene much. But I want to take is seriously, and I'm not looking to do anything that will screw it up."

Will raised both hands. "Sorry. I totally respect that. I'm happy for you. And whoever he is, he's a lucky man."

Roman took another sidestep. This had taken an uncomfortable turn. "Well, I hope I see you around. There's no reason we can't talk to each other, right?"

Will nodded, no longer smiling. "Better get going. It was nice seeing you." He hurried away before Roman could say anything more.

Awkward. Roman watched him walk, before suddenly realising just how cold he was. He stomped his feet to get the circulation going again and headed for home.

* * * *

When Roman reached the flat, he felt like the chill had entered his bones. Ashley was watching *The One*

Show in the living room. Roman pulled off his hat, scarf and gloves and rushed to the fireside to warm his hands on the gas flames. He shivered, barely able to feel the tips of his fingers.

"Working late again," Ashley remarked.

"I know. It's not great, but I don't know what else to do."

"They are taking the piss out of all of you. Any decent employer would either pay you for the overtime or insist you left at the end of your shift."

Roman didn't want to argue. Ashley failed to grasp the threat that loomed over him. Ashley had a secure civil service job in the waste department of the local council. He enjoyed thirty-three days of paid leave a year, flexitime, working from home two days a week and had every weekend off. He had no idea of the demands placed on workers in the private sector.

As the heat returned to his hands and his fingers began to throb, Roman turned around, hitched up the waist of his jacket and warmed his arse against the fire. "I think I'll get the bus home tomorrow if the weather doesn't improve." He rubbed his backside to get the blood flowing.

"It's not forecast to," Ashley said, turning down the volume on the TV and swinging his feet to the floor. "I need to talk to you about something."

"Sounds ominous," Roman said, finally unfastening his jacket.

"You're not going to like it."

"Ah, shit. Can't it wait until I've had something to eat? It's been a long day."

Ashley glanced at his watch. "Not really. That's why I hoped you'd get home earlier than this." He took a long, dramatic pause and exhaled before saying, "Patrick is coming by at eight."

Roman groaned and walked away. He took off his jacket and hung it on the stand in the hall. Ashley followed him to the kitchen, but Roman didn't want to look at him.

"What do you want me to say?" He pulled the pot of leftover pasta from the fridge and loosened the lid before putting it in the microwave. "The man's a violent, bad-tempered prick, unless you've forgotten. He took his fists to both of us. I certainly remember that. You told me you were done with him."

"I saw him last weekend," Ashley said, leaning against the counter with his arms folded. "I didn't say anything because I knew you wouldn't like it, but he asked if I would hear him out."

"He. Punched. Me." Roman said, accentuating every word.

"He's sorry for that. He couldn't have been more apologetic. He's destroyed by what he did."

"Don't tell me. *He's changed.*"

"Actually, he has. He knows his drug-taking had gotten out of hand, and he's addressed it. He's stopped it all — the steroids, the coke, the Es. He hasn't even had a drink since before Christmas. Patrick is a different person when he's sober."

"I wouldn't know," Roman said, getting a bowl from the cupboard and fork. "I've only ever seen him high."

"That's what I'm getting at. You don't know him, not really. You've only seen him at his worst. He's trying to be a better person."

Roman sighed. "Why are you telling me this? It's clear you've made up your mind to take him back."

"I think he deserves a second chance."

"Good for you," he bit.

"Don't be like that."

Roman struggled to keep a lid on his temper. "Oh, I'm sorry. Forgive me if I'm not ready to forgive the hulk who punched me in the stomach."

"He's really sorry." Ashley's voice pitched into an irritating whine. "He almost cried when we spoke about it. He wants to make it up to you, if you'll give him a chance to say sorry."

"No."

The microwave pinged. Roman grabbed the plastic bowl, stirred the steaming pasta and tipped it into his dish.

"C'mon. Don't be like that. At least give him the chance to apologise."

Roman was close to losing it. He didn't want to fall out with his flatmate, but this sudden U-turn on his toxic ex was pushing him. "No. Not a chance. Not now or ever. The man is a complete twat, and I don't want to waste another minute of my life on him. And I'm really surprised at you falling for his bullshit again. Isn't it bad enough that we can't walk around town without the fear that something bad will happen? There are people out there who want to seriously hurt us. No, not hurt, *kill* us. This is our home, Ashley. This is the one place we should feel safe. And you're going to open the door to a man who has harmed us both and ruin that."

Ashley's mouth dropped.

Before he could say another word, Roman picked up his dinner and took it to his room. He was afraid if he hung around, he would say something he would seriously regret.

* * * *

Half an hour later he could hear them in Ashley's room. At least Ashley had the sense to take him in there and not let the bastard longue around the flat like he owned the place. That would come soon enough if Ashley didn't grow a brain cell. Roman tried to watch TV but couldn't concentrate. All he could think about was the monster in the next room.

When his phone pinged a text alert, he snatched it, grateful for any distraction.

It was Mallon.

Hey, just got in. You busy? Want to come over?

He perked up. He hadn't expected to hear from him so soon. When they'd seen each other at the weekend, Mallon had warned him he had a heavy week coming up and wouldn't have much free time.

Before he could reply, the phone sounded another alert. It was a multimedia attachment. When the image of Mallon's beautiful hard cock filled his screen, Roman stiffened in instant arousal.

He keyed in a hasty response.

On my way.

Fuck Ashley and Patrick. Though he was furious to be driven from his own home, there was no one better than Mallon for him to run to.

Chapter Twelve

A Treat for Mallon

Mallon opened the door in just a pair of dark trousers and a white shirt, open to the chest. He was barefoot and looked hotter than the Sahara. He grabbed Roman by his jacket and hauled him inside, going straight for a deep, opened-mouthed kiss. Roman wrapped his arms around his strong back and responded, pushing his body against Mallon.

They parted breathlessly.

"Nice welcome," Roman said.

Mallon closed and locked the door.

Roman put down his overnight bag and had just removed his jacket when Mallon grabbed him from behind and ground his hard cock against his butt. He slid his hands beneath Roman's sweater, caressing his bare abdomen. He nuzzled his earlobe with his mouth.

"I'm hungry," Mallon said, "for you."

Roman raised his arms as Mallon pulled the sweater over his head. He wore a white T-shirt underneath, which came off, too. Mallon hugged him tight, his hands going straight to Roman's chest. His nipples were already hard from the sub-zero temperature outside. Mallon murmured appreciatively, squeezing and stretching the tips between his thumbs and fingers. He pressed his moist lips against Roman's neck, and when he shivered, it had nothing to do with the cold.

All Roman's anxieties about work, about Ashley and Patrick, were forgotten as Mallon became the only important thing in his world.

"I've got something to show you," Roman said, arching backwards as Mallon gently nipped his shoulder with his teeth.

Mallon hands slipped all over his torso, exploring his chest, belly, his flank. Stroking, caressing. "What is it?"

"Something I think you'll like."

"Don't tease. Show me."

"Take a seat."

Mallon kissed his neck again, before picking up his drink and carrying it to the longue area. He sat on the sofa. The bulge of his cock was obvious in his dark trousers.

Roman took his time, unfastening his boots and removing his thick socks. He wore another lighter pair underneath. He rose slowly, taking his time, drawing it out. Mallon's eyes followed every move he made, seemingly entranced. Roman savoured the power. He knew exactly what Mallon wanted, what buttons to press to turn him on. He unbuckled his belt, then the top button of his jeans. The second, then the third. He heard the quickening of Mallon's breath. He took a slow sip of red wine, keeping his eyes fixed on Roman.

Roman unbuttoned his jeans all the way and turned around. He paused, drawing it out before making the reveal. His own pulse was racing. He knew the impact this would have on his lover and what would follow. He pushed his jeans over his arse, exposing what was underneath.

He had bought the underpants two years before when he'd been in an especially horny mood and had only worn them once since — a pair of tight-fitting black trunks with a huge panel missing from the back that exposed his arse entirely. He'd seen loads of guys wear similar outfits while they cruised the arches at The Viaduct, but Roman had never felt that comfortable wearing them. When he'd tried them on at home, they had seemed kind of silly. But now, with an appreciative audience, he felt hot and empowered. He let his jeans rest at midthigh, and ran both hands over his buttocks, thrilling to the touch of bare, exposed skin.

Mallon released a deep groan. "Take the jeans off."

Roman shucked them to his ankles and hauled them off, standing before Mallon in just his socks and backless pants, exposing his juicy arse. "Do you like them?"

"Very much. Walk around the table. Let me see how your ass moves in them."

Roman obeyed, circling the coffee table. The front of the trunks swelled with his erection, but that wasn't what interested Mallon. He was a pure arse-man, and Roman gave him exactly what he wanted. Despite his lean build, his arse was oversized and out of proportion. The trunks only accentuated that further. Mallon chewed his bottom lips and stroked his cock while his eyes were glued to every move Roman made.

"You have more like this?" Mallon asked.

Roman shook his head. "Just a couple of jockstraps."

"I will buy you more. You shouldn't wear anything other than pants like this. Your arse should always be on display…always ready."

He chuckled. "I think they might have something to say about that at the office."

"Then they are idiots. Your ass is beautiful. These pants give it the justice it deserves."

Roman moved closer to him on each circuit of the table. Mallon stiffened and leaned forward, and as Roman came around again, he held out a hand to stop him. Roman didn't need to be told what to do next. He turned, presenting his butt, pressing it inches from Mallon's face. He heard Mallon take a deep inhalation and mutter something in French he didn't understand.

Then Mallon's hands were on his waist, pulling him closer. His breath was hot against Roman's buttocks, his nose brushed against the crack. Roman widened his feet, strengthening his posture. He put his hands on his thighs and pressed backwards. Mallon grabbed him, and with an animalistic groan, he buried his face in the crevice, his talented tongue going straight for the prize.

He ate Roman's hole till it was wet and ready, before standing up and pushing him face down onto the sofa. Mallon pulled a sachet of lube from his pocket and tore into it, before fingering Roman's hole, preparing the deeper passage. Then he was on top of him. Roman bore the weight on his back as Mallon shoved his trousers down and guided his sticky dick to the opening. He lined it up and shoved in. They groaned together. Roman gritted his teeth in pleasure as Mallon stretched and filled him. He would never get tired of this. There was an urgent need in both of them. They bucked and pushed against each other, both grinding and urging the other to fuck harder and take it deeper.

There was a cushion right beneath Roman's hips, and he rubbed his cock against it as Mallon pounded him from behind.

Mallon's breath hissed in his ear. "Going to come."

His fucking became more erratic. Roman thrust faster against the cushion. Their cries reached a crescendo, and they came together. As Mallon came inside Roman, Roman shot into the front of his briefs, filling them with his hot load.

"Wow," he gasped afterwards. Mallon remained inside him; his breath rasped against the side of Roman's head.

"Exactly," Mallon groaned and laughed. "I've been thinking about fucking you all day."

"You have?" Roman was surprised to hear Mallon thought about him at all when they were apart.

"I woke up this morning after having had a dream about you. A hot dream. Your ass has been on my mind ever since. It's been quite a distraction." He eased back gently, withdrawing.

Roman rose onto his knees. Mallon sat on the sofa with his trousers around his ankles, his cock glistening and semi-hard. He reached for the glass of wine and took a sip, gasping afterwards.

"The bottle is open on the counter," Mallon said. "Help yourself."

"I will. I'll just clean up first."

Roman grabbed his clothes and his bag and went to the bathroom. As well as a change of clothes so he could go straight to work in the morning, he'd brought some toiletries and a couple of spare sets of underwear. He took off the backless pants, which were now soiled with cum, and wiped himself down.

Mallon had pulled up his trousers and fastened his shirt when Roman returned to the main room. He poured a glass of wine and joined him on the sofa. He checked the time. *Nine-thirty.*

"Have you eaten?" he asked.

"Had something at the office this afternoon. You?"

Roman hadn't touched the pasta he'd reheated for dinner. He'd been too pissed off with Ashley to eat then. "I'm starving."

Mallon picked up his phone. "I'll order a takeaway, though it's probably too late to get something decent."

"Don't go to any trouble."

"What do you like?"

"Nothing you'll approve of, I'm sure. Pizza. Burgers. Curry. Chinese food. Fish and chips. I'll eat anything."

Mallon grimaced, scrolling through his phone. "Pizza is the least horrible of those options."

Roman laughed and leaned into him. "If I'd known I was coming over, I would have picked up food at the supermarket. I'm not the greatest cook, but I can do something special with a couple of chicken breasts — nothing fancy like you're used to, but better than a takeaway."

Mallon kissed the top of his head. "You think I'm a snob."

"I never said that."

"You don't have to say it. I know you do. It's okay. I am a snob about certain things. I'm not ashamed of it. Who would be proud of having horrendous taste, anyway? Ham and cheese okay for the pizza?"

Roman's favourite was chicken and mushrooms, but he suspected that might tip Mallon over the edge. "Whatever suits you is good for me."

Mallon tapped in the order and put down the phone. Unlike most people he knew, Mallon did not seem obsessed with his phone or social media. He only used it for calls or practical tasks like ordering food. It made a refreshing change. Roman had known men who made no secret of looking for their next hook-up while they were still with him.

This was more than a hook-up. Hook-ups were quick and casual. They didn't give you drinks or take you for breakfast or order pizza. *So what is this, exactly?* Roman wasn't sure. *Too early to put a label on it.* He should enjoy these moments for what they were and not build up his expectations.

"How was work?" he asked.

Mallon tutted. "No work talk. I've been at it all day and will be there again tomorrow. This is time to relax."

"Okay. Fair point. What do you do to relax?"

"I fuck you," Mallon said, playfully squeezing him.

"Apart from that. You must like doing something."

"I like all kinds of things. I go to bootcamp at six a.m. twice a week."

"That sounds like the opposite of relaxing."

"I like swimming, boxing. I'm interested in history." He gestured at two books on the coffee table. "After what you said the other day about Blyham, I decided I should know more. One book is the history of the city, and the other is a history of the northeast area. There's even a small chapter on your hometown. Nyemouth, right? I read about it last night."

"That can't have taken long," Roman said. "There's nothing there."

"It looks wonderful to me. I plan to visit while I'm here—maybe in the spring, when it's warmer."

"Oh, God yes. That place is bleak in winter. Best avoided." He snuggled in, catching on something Mallon just said. "Spring. So, you intend to still be here?"

"I should be here for most of the year, at least. This project won't get done overnight."

Roman smiled. "I hope you won't get tired of fucking me if you're staying that long."

Mallon hugged him tight. "Are you kidding? With that ass, I won't ever get tired of fucking you."

Roman flushed with pleasure. "How about we get together this weekend? I've got some more underwear you might like to see."

Mallon put his arm around him and squeezed his shoulder. "I'd love to, but I can't. I'm going home on Friday. I won't be back for at least a week."

Roman hid his disappointment. It wouldn't do to look too clingy. "Maybe next week, then?"

Mallon pulled him closer. His mouth was on top of Roman's and when he whispered, his breath was hot and exciting. "No need to wait so long. What are you doing on Thursday night? I have an idea that just might turn you on."

Chapter Thirteen

Return to The Viaduct

The heat and funk of The Viaduct took Roman in a familiar embrace. He had stood in line in sub-zero conditions for over ten minutes before reaching the front. With getting up early for work every Friday, he had yet to experience The Viaduct on a Thursday and was surprised to find it was the busiest night of the week. It was almost ten-fifteen when he got through the queue, paid the entrance fee and reached the changing room.

The theme for the evening was underwear or nothing.

The door attendant had given him a clear plastic bag for his clothes. Seven other men were undressing when he entered. Roman took off his scarf, gloves and coat, stealthily watching to see how far the others would go. A stunning Black man in his forties stripped to a grey jockstrap. His body was well-muscled, beefy rather than ripped, with a broad, hairy chest. The pouch of his jock struggled to contain his arousal. When he turned around, the rear displayed the most spectacular bare arse, wide and meaty, like a rugby player. Another man, late thirties, gym-perfect, went fully naked. His dick was on the small side, bolstered by a leather cock-strap, but from the way he arched his back and popped his hips, his cock was not on the menu. It was alpha bottom behaviour.

The rest of the men undressed to their underwear. They mostly wore boxer-briefs with trendy names blazed across the waistband. Their bodies ranged from skinny to muscled to big. As they went into the bar, more newcomers took their place.

Roman had visited the city centre sex shop on his lunch break yesterday to buy his costume for the evening. Given the excitement his backless pants had triggered in Mallon earlier in the week, Roman had known exactly what to choose—a pair of red briefs, cut away at the back to expose his arse. They weren't quite a jock strap. From the front, it appeared he was wearing a regular pair of pants, but when he turned around, there were his buttocks in their naked glory. The briefs went perfectly with his black, leather walking boots.

He bagged up his clothes and handed them to the attendant in exchange for a numbered wrist band and a token.

"That will get you one free drink," the attendant, a friendly looking middle-aged bear told him. "Anything else, run a tab on your wrist band and settle the bill when you collect your stuff at the end of the night."

Roman thanked him, familiar with the process, and moved through to the main bar.

It was packed. The warmth and scent from so many bare bodies was intoxicating. He'd never seen the place so full, not even on Saturdays. He wondered if the underwear theme was the most popular of their events? Or had the implicit danger of taking a stranger home for sex brought the crowd in? It might not be private, but in here they could fuck whoever they wanted, knowing there was safety in numbers.

He pressed his way to the bar, sliding against naked flesh, already slick and smooth with sweat. Heavy techno blared from the speakers, and the porn that played on the TV screens was hardcore fetish stuff, all leather and stretched holes. When it was his turn to be served, he exchanged the token for a vodka and Coke, the most expensive drink he could get for free. Later, when he had to pay for his drinks, he would switch to the cheaper beer.

He found a space against the wall where he could lean on the shelf to have his vodka. It was against the rules to take glasses and bottles up to the cruising areas.

The soft material of his underpants was surprisingly stimulating against his crotch. It grazed his cock and balls like silk. He had tried them on briefly last night, but wearing them properly for the first time, walking and moving around, was an unexpected thrill. Despite the cold outside, he'd had a semi-erection all the way here, and now he was in the club, it had grown to a raging boner. Together with the exposure of his arse, they were the sexiest pants he'd ever worn.

Eyes were on him. Hungry faces watched from all directions, checking out his cock and butt. Roman took a deep swallow. *Let them look.* Mallon treated him like the hottest young man in Blyham. Displayed and aroused in his new pants, he felt that way, too. The same men wouldn't have looked twice at him in his student days, when he was thin and awkward, with a gaunt face that didn't really suit him. Other gays bitched about getting old, about their need for Botox and other treatments to fight time, but Roman knew he had gotten better with every year.

At thirty-eight, Mallon was living proof that men could get more handsome and desirable as they aged.

Roman was just beginning. He would embrace maturity, not fight it.

He knocked off his drink, unable to contain himself any longer. He'd been hot with anticipation from the second he'd woken up that morning.

He pressed back into the crowd, pushing towards the stairs. Anonymous hands groped as he passed. They grabbed his hard cock, patted his buttocks, someone was bold enough to slip their fingers into the crack, aiming for his hole. He ignored the unwanted attention. His exposure gave them an invitation to look and nothing else. They could keep their dirty hands to themselves. He shook them off and moved on.

The upper playroom area was even busier than the bar, but it was bigger, making it easier to move around. Bare, sweating bodies were entwined, heaving together, illuminated by the sleazy red lighting. Though the techno music played, it was not as loud up here. Cries of ecstasy, guttural pleasure and the persistent slap of skin against skin dominated.

The room reeked of sex, of sweat and cum, arse and poppers. He breathed it in deep, intoxicated by the pungent baseness of it all.

There were eyes all over him, just like below. With his chin held high, Roman prowled through the massive room, stepping around men as they kissed and groped each other. More hands reached for his arse and tried to grab his bulge. When he moved away from them, they didn't follow. It was a clear rule of The

Viaduct that all attention should be warranted, and no meant no without exception.

The sling had a sizeable crowd gathered around it. Heads were bowed, watching, and the jerking of their shoulders gave away what was happening. He couldn't see the recipient of all that interest, but the suspension chains swung back and forth, and someone clearly shouted, "Yes. Yes. Fuck me. Fuck me more."

Roman's cock swelled harder than ever. He wondered what it would be like submit so thoroughly, to surrender his body for the pleasure of so many men — to take them on without a care for who they were or what they looked like, all comers welcome. It was a dark fantasy, one he'd gotten off to more than once. He was no stranger to threesomes, hooking up with couples when the time and combination was right, but he doubted he was uninhibited enough to act out his gangbang dream.

Not that he needed to when a man like Mallon could fuck him harder and better than all those guys put together.

He continued across the floor, making for the vaults. The corridor was thronged on either side. Guys edged the walls, presenting themselves, their faces filled with expectation. They stared at Roman as he passed, tugging their cocks through their underpants, showing how turned on they were. The sexual tension was heavy, almost palpable. Roman's cock strained against the pouch of his new pants. He'd created a damp patch of pre-cum already and hadn't engaged in a single act yet.

When strong arms wrapped around his torso, a chest pressed against his back, a hard cock against his buttocks, he didn't resist. The touch and smell were already so familiar. He leaned into the man who held him.

"What kept you?" Mallon growled in his ear, nipping the lobe with his teeth.

Roman shuddered. The place was sweltering, and still his body rippled with gooseflesh.

He arched his neck, turning his head towards Mallon. He reached behind to touch him, discovering bare flesh. Mallon had chosen to ignore the underwear theme in favour of full nudity. Mallon pulled him tight, pressing their bodies together.

"I like what you're wearing," Mallon said, and licked the sweat from his neck.

"I wore it for you," Roman gasped.

Mallon's fingers were on his nipples. He rolled and squeezed, sending pleasure all through his torso as the tips hardened to his touch. Through half-lidded eyes he caught the attention they were drawing. Guys turned to watch them, stroking their cocks with open intent. One man, thick-set and completely naked except for a leather mask that covered his entire head, took himself in both hands, squeezing his balls with one hand while working his shaft with the other. Another man tugged his erection free of his boxer-briefs. He licked his palm before getting to work on his dick, staring at Roman the whole time.

It shouldn't have been so arousing, but it was — being watching, knowing they were turning these other guys on.

Mallon steered him to one of the arched chambers. It was empty inside, apart from a padded bench. There was a curtain that could be drawn for privacy. Roman tingled with excitement when Mallon left it open.

"Do you want them to see us?" Mallon asked.

He nodded, unable to speak.

Mallon let go of him, backing away to lean against the wall. His handsome features were strong in the shadowy red light. "Turn around and let me see you."

Roman did what he'd asked. They had fallen into a hot routine, Mallon telling him what to do and him obeying without question. It was nothing deep, like BDSM, just something extremely erotic and sensual. Roman loved to please him.

Mallon looked like a God. His perfect physique glistened with sweat beneath the red lights. He grinned lasciviously, staring at Roman's new underpants, distorted completely by his raging hard on. Mallon was naked, apart from black leather construction boots and a steel cock-ring. The shaft of his cock throbbed with engorged veins, the head wet and shiny, and his ball sack, lifted by the ring, was full and jutted forward from his hips. As Roman feasted his eyes on his dick, Mallon twitched it.

"It's all for you," he said. "I've been waiting for you."

Roman dropped to his haunches and cupped his hand around Mallon's balls. The sack was tight and full. He squeezed gently before going in with his mouth. He drew his tongue along the smooth skin and inhaled the warm, musky scent of Mallon's groin. *Oh, yes.* The salty taste and ripe smell were intoxicating. He nuzzled the base of his cock with his nose but kept his primary focus on his nuts, opening his mouth to take one inside, applying the slightest amount of suction.

Mallon groaned, edging his hips forward while running his fingers through Roman's hair, caressing the back of his head in a motion that was both tender and passionate.

He released his ball and drew the other one inside, sucking a little harder this time. Mallon tightened his hold. Roman sucked deeper, until his heard a sharp hiss of breath, taking Mallon to the borderline of pleasure and pain. They were too big for him to take both balls in his mouth at once, so he alternated, sucking one then the other.

He was aware of a crowd closing in around them. He heard their murmurs of approval, the slick sound of their hands on their dicks. They could beat their meat as much as they wanted, but Roman's mouth was for Mallon's pleasure only.

He released his balls and moved up to his cock. Pre-cum drooled from the tip and down the shaft. It coated his tongue in its salty slick when he swallowed. Mallon tightened his grip on Roman's head, guiding the back-and-forth motion.

"Look at that slut. He fucking loves it," somebody said in a leering, overly loud voice.

Someone else sniggered.

Let them jeer. Roman was the one servicing the hottest man in the place. They were only jealous. He relaxed his jaw and took Mallon's dick all the way, letting it sit in his throat. It cut off his air supply. He held it for as long as he could, until his eyes watered, and he started to feel faint. He withdrew, choking, gasping.

"He's a real little pig," someone shrieked.

He worked Mallon's cock with devotion—deep throating, daring himself as he pressed his nose into his musky groin, against the cool steel of his cock-ring, to keep him inside for longer each time he swallowed. Mallon gripped a handful of hair and pulled him off.

"Enough. I want to show them your ass is mine."

Roman trembled with fresh excitement when Mallon reached into his boot and produced a sachet of lube. He nodded appreciatively and climbed onto the vinyl-covered bench, getting on all fours, and presenting his arse. Mallon tore into the sachet and emptied the contents into Roman's crack. Then his fingers got to work, massaging his opening, pushing the lube inside. One finger. Two. Three. Mallon drove into him with a smooth, twisting motion, ensuring he was fully prepared. Roman clawed at the vinyl surface, arching his back, and opening himself farther.

The entrance to the vault was packed. There were more men behind those who had the prime spots, standing on tiptoes to watch over their shoulders, obtaining a better view. He'd had sex in front of a couple of people before, but Roman had not been observed by so many. It was all-consuming.

The man in the leather mask was at the front, leaning against the stone archway, slowly stroking his dick. There was something unnerving about the mask. It covered his entire head, and the soft leather moulded to the features of the face. His eyes glinted through two open holes. The zipper across the mouth was undone, exposing his moist lips and bared teeth. Roman saw nothing mysterious or erotic about the hidden identity. It was frightening, like a killer in a slasher movie. He turned away, looking at the excitement he'd caused for the other, wanking men.

Mallon's cock pressed against his hole. This was it. Roman dropped to his elbows and lay his head on his forearms. Mallon pushed the head of his cock inside, then grabbed Roman's hips in both hands to drive it all the way. Roman sighed. The fullness of that cock completed him. *Mallon is in me. He's mine.*

Sweat poured over Roman's face as Mallon rode him. It stung his eyes. He licked his lips and tasted it. The men who watched grew more serious in their voyeurism. With their eyes fixed on Roman and Mallon, they tugged their balls and stroked their dicks with increasing force. The slap of Mallon's hips against his bare, upturned arse added to their groans of pleasure, along with the slick sound of hands upon cocks.

The back and forward friction of Mallon's dick was sweet bliss. Each deep thrust triggered greater ecstasy. Mallon gripped his hips tighter, and his pace became faster and more erratic. Roman recognised the signs.

Yes. Watch this, you bastards. Watch this man breed me.

Mallon pulled Roman's arse tight against his hips when he came. His cock pulsed and swelled as he spewed his load inside.

"Fuck, yeah," somebody called from the crowd.

Then something hot and wet splashed across Roman's shoulder. He opened his eyes to see that several of the observers had moved closer to the bench. A chunky bear had just shot over him. Another man, right in front, squeezed his balls and tilted his hips to unleash a gushing torrent across Roman's face. The man in the mask came next, depositing his cum over his back.

It was getting crazy. He hadn't asked for any of this. At the same time, he didn't want it to stop.

With his arse still rooted on Mallon's cock, Roman closed his eyes and let the cum spurt all over him.

* * * *

"Did you enjoy that?" Mallon asked.

He had closed the curtain, and they were alone in the vault. Outside, Roman heard the sex party continue in the surrounding rooms and corridors. Mallon sat on the edge of the cum-spattered bench, and Roman straddled his lap, with his arms around Mallon's neck. Mallon's hands held his arse, one finger gently massaging his tender, sloppy hole.

"I did," he admitted with a soft laugh.

He had wiped the cum from his face, but it seemed to be everywhere—in his hair, dribbling down his back.

"All that cum," Mallon said, pressing a kiss to his mouth. "For you. All those orgasms, all that pleasure. They did it for you. *I* did it for you."

"You knew I would like it?"

"I had a feeling you might."

"And you? Did you like them watching us?"

He shrugged. "Let them watch all they want. I'm the one who fucked you. They can come as much as they want, but they can't have what I have."

"It felt kind of dirty...in a good way."

"You're a dirty boy. You like to tease and show off your ass." He gave his butt a gentle slap. "I'm right, eh?"

Roman hugged him tighter. There was a slickness between their chests that could have been sweat or cum or both. He wriggled, smearing it between them. Their hard nipples rubbed together. "As long as I'm doing it with you, I'm game for anything."

Supporting his arse, Mallon stood. Roman wrapped his legs around his waist and tightened his grip on his neck to bear the weight. Mallon turned around and laid him down on his back. He gripped Roman's ankles and held them wide and open.

"This time it's just for me," he said.

With a smooth roll of the hips, he re-entered. Roman gasped, savouring the feeling of completeness again.

Chapter Fourteen

No Safe Haven

Though their bedrooms were separated by a hallway, Roman heard the raised voices from Ashley's room, and it was clear from the tone that he was arguing with Patrick. *Great.* They'd been back together for just over a week, and they were fighting already. It hadn't taken long for Patrick to drop the nice guy act and revert to his typical behaviour.

Patrick had been there when Roman had returned from work, sitting at the kitchen table with a shit-eating grin on his face while Ashley grilled a four pack of chicken breasts for him. Roman had said hello to Ashley and ignored Patrick completely, taking a bottle of beer from the fridge and going straight to his room. This couldn't continue. He was acting like a prisoner in his own home, afraid to use the shared communal areas. He would have to speak to Ashley when they were alone.

Roman was the one who shared the rent on this flat, not that meat-headed arsehole. Patrick had no right to behave like he owned the place.

Last week, Ashley had said Patrick wanted to say sorry for punching Roman last October. Roman was still waiting for the apology. He had no interest in speaking to Patrick, and the feeling was clearly mutual. He regretted not pressing charges against him after the assault. Back then, Ashley had assured him they were finished for good and involving the police would only prolong the agony of having Patrick in their lives. If he'd got the police to prosecute him, he could have taken out a restraining order and had him barred from the flat for good.

Roman couldn't face a night in listening to them fight. He changed out of his work clothes and put on jeans, a T-shirt and a warm sweater. He couldn't afford a big night out, but he'd rather go to the pub and spend what little money he had than suffer in silence here. Mallon had returned to France for the weekend and wasn't due back in Blyham until the middle of next week.

Roman knocked on Ashley's door a little before eight.

"Yeah," Ashley called from inside.

Heavy footsteps thudded across the floor, and the door jerked open. Patrick was stripped to the waist. His chest and arms were bigger than ever. His neck seemed to have disappeared, and his head was balanced on his wide shoulders. Ropey veins bulged all over his body. *So much for quitting the steroids.*

"What d'you want?" he asked. His jaw protruded as he chewed frantically at a piece of gum. His eyes were agitated, roaming over Roman's face.

And still no apology. Roman moved to one side, trying to see past him into the room. The lights were on low, and Patrick angled the door to block his view.

"We're busy in here?" he growled.

"Busy arguing," Roman said, refusing to back down. "Thin walls. Is everything all right?" he called over Patrick's shoulder.

"Yes, it's fine," Ashley said. Roman could not see him.

"Happy now?" Patrick glowered.

Roman ignored him. "Are you sure? I'm going out, but I'll stay if you want me to."

"It's fine. Really," Ashley said. "Go out. Have a great time."

Roman looked daggers at Patrick while addressing Ashley. "Okay. I won't be late. I've got work in the morning. But we need to talk this weekend. Okay?"

"What about?" Patrick asked, standing over him.

Roman didn't back down. "House rules," he said defiantly.

"No problem," Ashley called. "I'll see you tomorrow after work. Have a good night."

Patrick sneered, showing his ugly little teeth before shutting the door in Roman's face.

* * * *

"You should have called the police when you had the chance," Phil said. "You had plenty of witnesses to back you up."

"I realise that now," Roman said.

He sat at the end of the bar in Julie's. For a Friday night, the place was quiet. Phil expected it to fill up after ten, though that seemed optimistic. When the Uber had brought him here, Roman had not seen many people on the streets. The cold weather, combined with a post-Christmas January slump and the on-going threat of the Blyham Strangler kept them away.

There were a handful of customers in the beer garden and another twelve or so smattered about the pub. Before the troubles, this place would have been packed.

Roman finished the beer he had made last almost an hour and raised the empty bottle to show he wanted another.

"The man has always been trouble," Phil continued, setting the new drink in front of him. "I still won't allow him in here."

"Really?"

"Absolutely. He's barred for life. Anyone who raises a fist to one of my customers gets the same treatment. There are no second chances for the kind of people who resort to violence. And from what I've heard of Patrick, he's got a long history of it."

Phil moved along the bar to serve a couple of women who had just come in, shivering from the cold. Phil was a nice guy. Why couldn't Ashley fall in love with someone like him instead of a toxic prick like Patrick? Phil was nearly forty, probably ten years older than Ashley, but he was in great shape, a hundred percent better looking than Patrick and far more chilled and intelligent. The age difference wouldn't matter at all. Ashley had told him before that he fancied Phil. He wondered if the attraction was mutual. If he could get them to take notice of each other, Ashley might realise what a complete loser Patrick was.

Not that it should take a genius to figure that out. Anyone with half a brain could see what a piece of shit he was.

Phil returned to his end of the bar. "You need to have it out with Ashley. You can't continue to live there and hide in your bedroom. It's your flat as much as it is his."

"Believe me, I intend to. I want to have that conversation tomorrow, if he doesn't find a way to squirm out of it."

"Tell him if he wants to see Patrick, they need to go to his place instead."

"I'm not sure I can go that far. Ashley pays half the rent, too. He has a right to do what he wants in his own home."

Phil picked up a tea towel and started polishing glasses from the upper shelves. "Then he should be more considerate."

"That's just it. He is. Ninety-nine per cent of the time he's the most perfect flatmate. He cleans up after himself, does his share of chores, doesn't play his TV or music too loud. We get on brilliantly. But when it comes to Patrick, his brain turns to shit. For whatever reason, he's infatuated with him."

Phil grimaced. "If Patrick had a single redeeming feature, I could understand it. But he doesn't. Looks, personality, kindness? He's a failure on every front."

Roman was ready to change the subject. He'd come to the pub to get away from Patrick, not talk about the fucker all night. "Has there been any more trouble these last few days?" he asked.

Phil nodded. "Another week, another shit storm. A couple of lads were harassed on their way back to their hotel last weekend. Visitors from Derby so they had no idea of the circumstances. They didn't know it wasn't safe to walk around at night. As far as I'm aware, it was verbal abuse and nothing violent happened, but they were all over social media afterwards, slagging the city off and saying they would never come back. Can't say I blame them. If I didn't already live here, Blyham would be at the bottom of my list of places to visit."

Roman stared grimly into his drink while Phil served more customers. He loved his life in Blyham. He couldn't think of another northern city where he would rather be. Newcastle, Leeds, Manchester, they all had their merits, but none of them compared to Blyham. From starting university, when he'd sampled the nightlife for the first time, he had known that he belonged here.

But for how much longer?

That was a question he had no answer to.

Would the city be the same after everything that had happened in the last year? Maybe it would bounce back once The Strangler was caught, maybe it wouldn't. The venues around the gay village occupied places of prime real estate. There had been rumours going around for years that the city council was interested in driving out the LGBTQ businesses and gentrifying the area. The murders might be just the reason they needed to close the place down. The Viaduct, with its reputation for men-on-men sex had long been at the top of the hitlist.

What were the chances that Roman would even be here once it was over? If his circumstances didn't change quickly, they were slim. And what about Mallon? He said he'd be here for a few months, but there had been no great commitment from him about that. Would Mallon be interested if he were living at home with his parents? *Hardly*. What grown man would be?

Fuck. Roman felt more depressed than ever.

"Can I have a double a vodka and cola?" he asked Phil, counting the change in his wallet. He'd have enough for one more drink after this, then he'd have to call it a night.

"Drowning your sorrows?" Phil asked as he poured the order.

"Getting that way. I'm struggling to think of much to be grateful for."

Phil rolled his eyes. "Drama queen. Tell Ashley to get his sleazy boyfriend out of the flat, and your troubles are over."

"That's not everything. I wish it was." He told him about his money worries and the looming threat of redundancy. "I must have written to every accountancy firm in the city with my CV in the last year. None of them are hiring. If I lose this shitty job, I don't know where I'll find another one."

"If it helps, I'm hiring," Phil said. "It's not accountancy, and I can only offer a couple of shifts a week, but if you want to earn a little extra money and maybe save some of it for a rainy day, the offer is there."

"Seriously? I thought business was down."

"It is, but I'm still short. I need staff to run the place. I can't do everything on my own. Do you have you any experience of bar work?"

"Yeah. I had a second job all the way through university."

"Great. Well, just think of it like that, taking on a second job while things are tough."

Roman swallowed his drink, giving it some thought. "I'm not sure. It's been a while. I don't know if I can do it anymore." But he was already thinking ahead. As well as the extra cash coming in handy, it would get him out of the flat a couple of times a week and away from Patrick. He was already working several hours of free overtime. Wouldn't it be better to get paid for the extra work?

"How about a trial shift?" Phil suggested. "Come in on Sunday morning for eleven. I can show you the ropes while it's quiet, then we usually get busy from three onwards when the cabaret starts. What about doing eleven to seven? I'll pay you, too, even though it's a trial."

What did he have to lose? He had no plans for this weekend, Mallon was in France. If he hated it or sucked at it, he could walk away at the end of the shift with a few extra pounds and no commitment — or it could be great and might help him out of his financial hole.

"All right," he said, suddenly loving the idea. "If you're serious, I'd like to give it a try."

"You're on," Phil grinned. "Be here for eleven, and we'll take it from there."

* * * *

From the beer garden, a man had been watching Roman unnoticed for the last hour. By that time, the venue had filled up to near normal capacity.

Around ten-thirty Roman fastened his jacket and left the bar. The man slipped through the crowd and followed him outside.

Roman had already crossed the road and was walking up the street towards the town centre.

After everything that was going on, Roman was walking the street on his own again. The man couldn't decide if that made him incredibly brave or just plain stupid. Whatever, it excited him to see the young fool alone. The man pulled the peak of his cap over his brow wrapped his scarf around the lower half of his face and crossed to the other side of the road to follow him.

Roman had a brisk walk and quickly extended the distance between them. The man increased his own pace slightly. Not too much. He didn't want to draw attention. There was no need. He knew where to find Roman when he was ready. His time was coming. The man had wanted him for months and couldn't ignore the urge for much longer.

He'd spent weeks fantasying about the moment, the night when he would get Roman exactly where he wanted him, when he would pin his body to the bed and wrap his hands around his throat. How much pressure would it take? The man's cock grew hard at the thought. Would he put up much of a fight? Probably. Roman had a slender build, but there was strength behind it. It was obvious in the way he strode along the pavement tonight, the purpose with which he walked. It was not the gait or posture of a potential victim. Roman would be a challenge, and the man thrived on those.

His target turned the corner at the end of the road, heading for the taxi rank, no doubt.

The man hurried to catch up. He wanted one more glimpse of his future victim before quitting for the night.

As he rounded the street, he saw the taxi pick-up point was empty.

Fuck. Had he caught a cab so soon?

As the man looked along the road, he spotted Roman farther ahead, still on foot. *Interesting. Is he going to walk all the way home, despite the dangers in the city?*

The man followed, keeping a safe distance. He didn't want Roman to see him. Not yet. Tonight was not the night.

Roman paused when he reached the bus stop and turned. The man edged closer to the wall, keeping out of sight as Roman stuck out his hand to flag down an approaching bus.

Not a complete idiot.

He watched as the bus came to a stop and Roman boarded, paying the fee and finding a seat as it pulled away again.

The man's breath quickened and billowed around his head as Roman was carried out of sight.

That boy was the hottest thing in Blyham, so confident and assured in his sexuality. No one else came close. None of the men he'd killed so far had excited him in this way.

The man groaned and adjusted his hard on in his jeans.

Roman's time was coming to an end. It would not be long.

He would squeeze the life out of him and relish every delicious second.

Chapter Fifteen

A Grim Discovery

Roman was waiting at the front of Julie's at five minutes to eleven on Sunday morning. He had stayed home last night, watched an old Roger Moore Bond movie, avoided alcohol and gone to bed after ten. Phil was throwing him a financial lifeline, and he couldn't afford to screw it up. He had to take this trial seriously. Just a couple of shifts a week for the next few months would enable him to save money in a way he couldn't right now.

Ashley and Patrick had gone clubbing, which had been another incentive for Roman to stay home and savour the peace. He had yet to have the conversation he needed with Ashley. He knew he couldn't put it off much longer, but having the flat to himself and being able to enjoy an early night, just for once, had been a blessing. They had come in sometime around four. Roman had heard them in the kitchen — thankfully there were no arguments — and he'd been able to turn over and get right back to sleep. They were both still in bed with he'd left that morning.

Roman had already decided that if the conversation with Ashley didn't go the way he'd like it to, he'd have no choice but to move out. He could never afford a place of his own, but it was time to make enquiries and see if anyone was in the market for a flat share, preferably someone without a toxic boyfriend. The money he earned working at Julie's would come in handy for a deposit, should he need one.

He felt surprisingly cheerful this morning. A part-time job could be just what he needed. It was a progression. The first step on a journey, and it was something he was doing for himself. Nothing would change for the better if he sat around waiting for it. He had to take ownership of his situation. The job would mean less time to spend with Mallon, but it's not like they were living in each other's pockets, anyway. They only got together one or two nights a week and for a few hours at the weekend. And with Mallon returning to France at short notice, Roman couldn't allow his own life to revolve around the availability of his lover.

If Mallon really wanted to spend time with him, they would find a way.

Roman checked his watch. Two-minutes past eleven. He tried the door again. Still locked.

He had always imagined Phil to be efficient and punctual to a fault. He could get pretty pissy when people arrived late and delayed one of his meetings. *"Time waits for no one,"* he would often say.

Still, it was Sunday morning, and he would have been up late last night. The poor guy probably didn't get to bed until two or three. He was entitled to a lie in. Not everyone had the luxury of the early night Roman had enjoyed.

When the door was still locked at ten past eleven, Roman knocked. He hoped he hadn't got the wrong time. He was certain Phil had told him to come for eleven. Had he made a mistake? What if he'd said twelve? Even worse, what if he'd changed his mind? Phil said the bar was quiet. He might have done a check on the finances and realised he couldn't afford the extra help after all. *But no*, Roman thought. Phil would have called to let him know. He wouldn't have made him come down on a cold Sunday morning for nothing.

He must have slept in.

Roman checked his phone, searching for Phil's number when someone approached him from the right.

"Are the doors locked?" It was Kat, one of the regular bartenders. She had changed the colour of her short blonde hair since Roman had seen her last. It was now two-tone with streaks of white and royal blue.

"Yeah. I've been here fifteen minutes. There's no answer."

"He'll be in bed." Kat opened her oversized black leather handbag and rummaged inside. She seemed to reach to the bottom of the farthest corner before retrieving a huge set of keys. "It happens all the time. He gave me these in case I must open on Sunday. Most weekends I do."

Roman laughed, relieved. "Did Phil tell you I was coming?"

She nodded, frowning as she shifted through the selection of keys until she found the right one. "Yeah, he mentioned it. Trial shift, right? Don't worry. He'll be down to show you the ropes. Phil is quite keen on you, by the sound of it. We've struggled to retain good staff lately, and he seems to think you'll do a lot better.

You've done bar work before, right?" She unlocked the front door and entered.

"Only at uni." He followed her into the dim interior. How different Julie's appeared without the lights, the people, the music and atmosphere he was used to. He had a sense of trespassing, like he shouldn't be here. Even the smell of the place was different — the sourness of stale alcohol together with damp odour of the drains and cellar. "It's been a few years."

Kat locked the door behind them and led the way to the bar. "That's good enough. If you've got experience, you'll pick it up fast. Julie's isn't all that different from the student union bar. That's where I started, too, by the way."

"Have you worked here long?"

Kat had been as much a part of the place as Phil in all the time Roman had been coming here. "A little over two years, I think. The biggest problem I found — that I still have — is hearing the orders when the bar is jammed and the music is blasting, but even then you'll get good at lip-reading. I don't make that many mistakes these days." She chuckled and removed her coat. "This way. I'll show where you can leave your things."

She gave him a brief tour of the downstairs area. There wasn't much to see. Behind the bar there was a long stock room, with coat hooks on one wall and a tiny table with a kettle and pots of tea and coffee. "The cellar is down there," she pointed to a hatch. "I'll let Phil show you that part. I hate going down there. Cellars are just so creepy. And the ceiling is low, so you'll have to watch your head."

"I'll manage."

Kat returned to the main bar and turned on the overhead lights. "Were you out last night?"

"No. I stayed in, knowing I was coming here today."

"You won't have heard then? Another man was attacked at the far end of Broad Street."

He sighed. "Not another one."

Kat nodded grimly. "Badly this time, too. They had to take him away in an ambulance. Three fuckers laid into him with metal poles. They beat the poor fella to a pulp. That's what I've heard, anyway."

"Three?" Roman immediately flashed on the faces of the men who had attacked him last October. Were those same guys still cruising the streets, looking for new victims? If they were, their methods had escalated. And if they were out there every weekend, how the hell hadn't the police caught them yet? They were hardly lying low. "Bastards. Do you know who it was? The guy they assaulted?"

"No. A few names have been passed around, but there's nothing definite. I'm sure we'll find out later today." Kat switched on all the lights for the bar fridges. "Why don't you make a start filling these in? You'll find all the stock you need back there, and it will give you a chance to get used to where everything is. Beers, ciders, white wine are all in the chillers here. Spirits and mixers are either on the counter or in one of these lower cupboards. Take your time and get a feel for the place. I'm going upstairs to see what's keeping Phil. He's usually down by now. When I come back, I'll show you how the till works."

Roman nodded. He was already familiar with the layout of the fridges and stock in Julie's. He'd spent enough time standing at the bar waiting for drinks to get a good idea of where they kept everything. He found a notepad and pen beneath the counter and started compiling a list of what they needed. The fridges hadn't been restocked at the end of the busy Saturday night shift and were almost empty of bottled beer and cider. He scribbled down what was required and went into the stock room.

He found a mixed case of bottled cider and carried it back to the bar. The fridge shelves had all been carefully labelled, so it was easy to know what went where. *This isn't too bad*, he thought, remembering his time at the student union bar. Though he predominantly worked there for the cash, he had enjoyed it — the camaraderie of the staff, the banter with the customers. Tips had been a rarity, but he couldn't deny enjoying himself. He hoped that would also prove to be true of working here.

He already knew most of the staff by sight, if not by name. They were a friendly bunch, and he was sure he would fit in easily.

A loud scream from directly above caused him to freeze.

It sounded like Kat.

There came the thud of footsteps across the ceiling then another, more desperate scream.

"Roman. Oh, my God, Roman."

He put down a bottle and hurried across the bar. Kat had gone through a door in the corner of the stock room. It was open, and he followed into a dimly lit passageway. There were stairs to the left. Roman raced up, two steps at a time.

He found her on the landing. She was on her hands and knees, gasping for breath. There was barely any light. Four of the five doors that came off the landing were shut, with just a wedge of dull grey light coming from the open door. He scrabbled around the walls until he found a switch and turned it on. He dropped to his knees, beside Kat. Her entire body trembled when he laid a hand on her shoulder.

"What is it? What's wrong?"

Between gasping for breath, she made a strange, high-pitched keening noise. Roman had never seen anyone in this state before. Was she ill? Was she in shock? He glanced towards the open door but could see nothing inside beyond the bottom corner of a bed.

Ice cold fingers of dread skittered along his spine.

"Kat," he said, sounding calmer than he felt. "What is it?"

"Phil," she gasped between breaths. "He's in there… He's… I think he's dead."

Oh God. Panic surged all through his body and threatened to overtake him. He fought against it. Kat had lost it. He owed it to Phil to keep it together. "*I think he's dead,*" she had said. She didn't know. She wasn't sure. Phil could be ill. He might have had a heart attack. There was a chance it might not be too late.

Roman rose unsteadily. Kat was a mess, but she was breathing and making plenty of noise. She was all right for now. Phil was the unknown. Phil needed his attention.

He hurried to the bedroom door.

Roman knew, in the leaden grey light of the room, that it was too late.

The figure on the bed did not move. There was something eerily unnatural about the angle in which he lay. There were no sounds, no breathing. Roman moved his hand up the wall, searching for the light switch. He found it. He closed his eyes a millisecond before turning it on.

His heart pounded and seemed to fill his entire chest. He felt it was going to crush his lungs. *Open your eyes.* He hesitated. Couldn't do it. *Open your fucking eyes. You might still be able to help him.*

He inhaled and forced his lids apart.

Phil was naked on the bed with the covers twisted around his legs. One arm was splayed from his body, the other was twisted inwards, laying partly across his chest. There was blood on the sheets, between his thighs. His skin was a ghastly greyish-blue shade. Roman forced himself to look at his face, searching for any hint of life. Phil's slack jaw and open eyes, his swollen lips and tongue destroyed any hope Roman had of saving him.

He backed out of the room. On the landing he leaned against the wall for support. Kat was still on her knees. Her mouth was open, but no sound came out. Her grief-stricken face was colourless.

Roman fumbled in his pocket. When he pulled out his phone, his fingers could barely operate it. He had to call the police, but his mind and his body seemed unable to function.

Phil is dead. Oh my God, he's dead.

As he finally managed to dial the emergency number, Roman knew with absolute certainly that his friend had become the latest victim of the Blyham Strangler.

Chapter Sixteen

Another Victim

"There's nothing we can do," Roman said, crouching beside Kat. "We should wait downstairs. Come on."

When she didn't react, he put his hand on her shoulder and gently squeezed. It seemed to bring her back to the present.

He helped her to stand.

"Is he...?" she asked.

"Yes."

She let out another short shriek. Roman put his arm around her waist and guided her to the stairs. Staying strong for Kat kept him from crumbling himself. His mind kept returning to the sight of Phil on the bed, that ghastly expression on his face and the colour of his skin. He must have been dead for several hours.

"When did you see him last?" he asked, helping her down a step at a time.

"After two. We...closed the bar at one, cleared the mess up then stayed back for a couple of drinks. It's what we do every Saturday."

"Was he alone when you left?"

She sniffed and nodded. "He waited at the door until my Uber arrived then locked up behind me... Oh God." Her legs weakened. Roman held her tighter.

"Come on. Not far now." They reached the bottom of the stairs. He walked her through the bar, and they sat together on a sofa in the far corner.

"Any sign of a break-in?" Kat asked.

"I don't know. I haven't looked. The police said not to touch anything else until they arrive. We'll be okay to wait for them here, I'm sure."

"My bag," Kat said, flustered. "I need my bag." She made a move to stand and wobbled.

"I'll get it," he assured her, telling her to stay where she was until he returned. She had left it in the stock room and seemed fleetingly relieved when he gave it to her. She rummaged inside and pulled out a packet of tissues, offering one to Roman. He took it and realised for the first time that he was also crying. His hand shook as he wiped his eyes and cheeks.

"Do you think...it's him?" Kat gasped. "*The Blyham Strangler.*" She whispered the words.

"It's hard not to." He didn't know how much she had seen when she'd entered the room, but when Roman had turned on the light, it had left him in no doubt that Phil had been strangled. The expression on his face, his bulging tongue, his eyes... Choked in his bed, just like those other men. And there had been blood on the sheets, between his legs. He'd heard rumours, nothing but unsubstantiated gossip, that the strangler mutilated and degraded his victims after their deaths. Is that what he had done to Phil? A swell of sickness deepened in his stomach. Roman shuddered and said nothing. If Kat hadn't seen those awful details for herself, she didn't need to know about them now.

"Oh my God, Phil." She bawled openly, great sobs wracking her chest. "He's the nicest man I know. He would do anything to help anyone. Nothing was ever too much trouble. Who the fuck would want to hurt him?"

Roman held her as she cried. He didn't have the answers. Everything she said was true. Phil Logan was a great man and a good friend. Roman hadn't even known him for long, but in a short time, he had become a powerful ally.

And now he lay above them, cold in his bed.

The world had become an evil place.

Roman lost all sense of time. He had no idea how long had passed when they heard hammering at the pub door.

"Police," a voice called.

There were four uniformed officers on the doorstep. One of them came inside and spoke kindly to them. Roman struggled to focus on what he said, and the officer had to repeat himself twice.

"CID and the forensics team are en route," the officer said a second time. "My colleagues are going to secure the scene outside. What time is the bar due to open?"

Roman looked at Kat. She had stopped crying, but her eyes were raw, her face red and blotchy. "Soon," she sniffed and looked at her watch. "Ten minutes."

"Thank you," the officer said. "My colleagues will take care of that. In the meantime, I need one of you to show me the crime scene."

Kat gasped. Her hand flew to her mouth. "I can't go up there again."

"I'll show you," Roman told the officer, who looked even younger than he was. He wondered how he could be so calm in the face of such a devastating discovery. Roman led him to the upper landing. "He's in the room at the end. I can't go back in there," he said.

"Stay here," the young officer said. "I just need to make sure there's nothing we can do for him."

It took less than a minute for him to inspect the room. Roman heard him say something into his radio before coming back along the landing. "We can wait downstairs," the police officer said.

What came next was a confusing blur of activity. The policeman, Officer Burrows, took statements from Roman and Kat while a succession of teams arrived, in plain clothes, uniforms and forensic overalls. Other than Burrows, Roman had no idea who any of them were. Roman felt useless. He hadn't seen Phil since Friday night when he'd offered him the job, and there was little he could add to his statement.

He asked Kat if there had been any trouble the night before, whether there been any disgruntled customers? Did Phil have cause to throw anyone out? Was he in a relationship? Did he have any visitors?

Sometime later, Roman and Kat were still sitting in the bar when a familiar face walked through the door. Benito Copploa, his hook-up of a few weeks earlier who had turned out to be a police office on the Blyham Strangler case. Benito came into the pub and spoke to one of the PCs at the door, before looking over to Roman and Kat. He nodded and approached.

Roman got up to meet him.

Benito wore a charcoal three-piece suit with a blue shirt, pink tie and black, highly polished shoes. The suit looked sharp on his muscular frame. The last time

Roman saw him at the town hall meeting, he'd been pissed off to discover he was a secret police officer, but now he was grateful to see a reassuring face.

"How are you doing?" Benito asked.

Roman shrugged. "I don't even know. Shocked. Numb. It hasn't sunk it."

Benito's expression was full of sympathy. It struck Roman how incredibly handsome he was with his classic Italian good looks, and he rebuked himself for thinking about such a thing at a time like this. "Are you part of the investigation team? Into the Blyham Strangler?"

Benito winced. "I'd rather we didn't call him names like that, but yes, I'm on the major incident team for his case."

It struck him that Phil would have been furious with Benito. He had little time for the police anyway, let alone a gay officer who had failed to stop so many unnecessary deaths. But Roman didn't have it in him to be angry. Maybe later he would feel that way, but for now a deep sense of sadness made it impossible for any other emotion to break through.

"Don't you have any leads?"

"We'll need to conduct a thorough investigation here," Benito said. "Interview everyone who came in last night, check out the CCTV footage from the pub and the venues close by. How well did you know Mr Logan?"

"Not well enough," Roman said despondently. "I didn't even know that was his surname until this morning. But he's always been good to me, always supportive. That's the kind of man he was. He offered me a job when I needed it."

"Might someone have taken advantage of his good nature, used it as a means of getting closer to him?"

"I don't know. It's possible, I suppose, but I'm not sure how easily he would have fallen for anybody insincere. Phil had a highly attuned bullshit detector. He was no walkover. He was pretty clued in about people."

Benito nodded. "That's helpful. Thanks." His brown eyes connected with Roman's. They lingered a moment longer than necessary. "Do you still have my number?"

Roman flinched. "Sorry. I er...don't."

Benito opened his wallet and handed him a card. "It's all on there. Give me a call if you think of anything else that might be useful." He paused for a moment. "I'd love to hear from you."

Roman pocketed the card without looking at it. He couldn't decide if Benito was being friendly or a creep. Either way, the direction their conversation had taken made him uncomfortable. "I don't think there anything I can add to the statement I've already given. I'm only here today for a work trial. If it wasn't for that, I wouldn't have been here at all."

And Kat would have found Phil's body by herself. If there was any solace to be taken from this morning, it would have to be that.

* * * *

By five o'clock Roman had not been home. The police had finally released Kat and him after three, by which time news of Phil's murder had spread all through the village. Ashley met him at The New Inn, keen to buy the drinks and help to numb his pain. After four bottles of beer, Roman didn't feel anything other than numb. He guessed that was the whole point of Ashley's mission.

Ashley had not invited his toxic boyfriend, which was one thing Roman could feel grateful for. He couldn't deal with Patrick's bullshit…not today. Though it was just the two of them, they had barely been left alone the whole time they were there. Hordes of people passed by their table, keen to know what Roman had seen and what the police had told him. He found the attention sickening. These people seemed more interest in hearing the grim details than paying any kind of respect to Phil.

"I always thought the two of you would have made a nice couple," Roman told Ashley, as he started on his fifth beer.

"Who? Me and Phil?"

"Yeah. He's a nice guy. *Was* a nice guy. Really nice. You could have done a lot worse. You *have* done a lot worse."

Ashley swigged his beer and let Roman's shady remark slide. "I don't think we ever fancied each other. Phil was a hottie for an old guy. I fancied him for a while, but I don't think he ever looked at me that way. I enjoyed his company, but there was never any spark between us. I don't think it would have worked out."

"We'll never know now," Roman said, glaring at the scratch marks on the wooden table. Ordinarily the jukebox would have been playing by this time on a Sunday afternoon, but the manager had left it switched off, allowing the customers some quiet time to reflect on the friend they had lost and the shock that another member of their community had fallen victim to the killer who hunted them. Roman ran his hands across his face. Would he ever rid himself of the sight he'd seen in Phil's bedroom? Right now, it was seared into the insides of his eye lids. When he closed his eyes, Phil's face was the only thing he saw.

"I forgot to mention," Ashley said, changing the subject. "Mallon is back from France."

Roman looked up. He rested his elbows on the table, his chin in his hands. "He is?"

"You didn't know? Thought not. You'd have mentioned it otherwise."

"What makes you sure?"

"I saw him." Ashley covered a belch with his fist.

"When?"

"This morning. Patrick and I went for a late breakfast along the riverside. You know the place with the blue sign and the high tables outside? There. He came in for a coffee around noon."

"You're sure it was him?" Mallon hadn't given him a date for his return from France, but Roman had taken it for granted that he would get in touch when he did. He even thought Mallon would have texted him a day or two in advance.

"It was him. I know what he looks like. Besides, I heard him speak. French accents aren't all that common around here."

Roman didn't know what to make of the news. He was disappointed that Mallon couldn't be bothered to let him know he was back in Blyham. Mallon mustn't think as much of Roman as he did of him. *Does it even matter?* After what had happened today, Roman didn't have the energy or inclination to worry about his love life. Until now, he'd though Mallon was one of the most important things he currently had going on, but the memory of Phil lying lifelessly in bed put that is perspective.

Fuck him.

Mallon would be in touch when he got horny, and maybe Roman wouldn't be so willing to drop his pants and bend over when he did.

"Have you ever wondered about him? This Mallon guy?" Ashley asked.

"What do you mean?"

"Well, you hardly know anything about him at all, do you?"

"We haven't known each other for long. It takes time."

Ashley shook his hand. "I don't mean where does he come from, or what's his favourite colour. I mean have you ever seriously wondered about him?"

"I don't know what you're getting at."

He gave a deep dramatic sigh. "Well, think about it, just for a minute. Who has been in town at the time of the last two murders that we know of? He has."

Roman tutted. "So were we, and everyone else we know."

"But we know we're not serial killers. He could be. And we know he wasn't with you last night or when Cameron was murdered. It could be him. What if the Blyham Strangler is actually the French Strangler? You should find out where he was at the time of all the other murders. It could be important."

"You're being ridiculous now. I'm not going to ask him any of that."

"Then don't blame me when you wake one night to find his hands around your neck."

"You'll be entirely blameless. Don't worry about that."

Ashley was being overly dramatic, as usual. Roman had no concern that Mallon was dangerous or The

Strangler, but he was a dark horse all right. He wanted Roman available at the click of his fingers but was unwilling to reciprocate. The bastard couldn't even tell him he was back in town. Roman needed to take stock of his life, and if that meant not jumping when a sullen Frenchman demanded a booty call, then things could only get better.

He raised his empty beer bottle. "I've had it with this stuff. I need something stronger. I'm getting a vodka. What do you want?"

Ashley shrugged. "The same."

Roman saw no better prospect than getting shitfaced tonight. The alcohol would numb his pain and might help with the nightmare visions that haunted him. It was better than nothing.

He got up and walked unsteadily to the bar.

Chapter Seventeen

"Don't say it's over."

Roman's mother sent a text early on Monday morning to tell him she was coming to Blyham. When he explained he had to go to work, she made arrangements to meet him at lunchtime in a coffee shop close to his office. Despite the alcohol he'd consumed the day before, his low mood had nothing to do with his hangover. He'd had a fitful, nightmare-plagued sleep, and when he woke up, all he could think about was Phil's lifeless body on the bed.

His mother was waiting when he entered the coffee shop just after one and leapt to her feet, hauling him into a tight embrace. "Oh, son, you look terrible. Have you even slept?" She pressed kisses to the side of his head, the way she used to do when he had been little.

"I did, yes." A lie, but the truth was something he didn't want to discuss.

She stepped back to look him over more carefully. "You're ill. The shadows under your eyes are as black as coal. You shouldn't be at work today."

"I didn't have a choice. I had to go in."

She furrowed her brow. She seemed on the verge of making an argument before she apparently softened her stance and tried a different approach. "Then you need to eat. Sit down, and I'll order for you. You need feeding up as well as everything else." She picked up her purse and went to the counter without asking him what he wanted.

Sophie Ballentyne was a no-nonsense woman of forty-nine. She had been a nurse at the local hospital for as long as Roman could remember, and the firm-but-fair attitude she delivered to her patients was mirrored in her parenting. Roman didn't argue with her. Right now, he realised he needed some of those home comforts.

He checked his phone while he waited for her to return, but still no messages from Mallon. There was nothing to stop him from calling Mallon himself, but given how the Frenchman hadn't bothered to tell him he was back in the UK, Roman didn't see why he should make the first move.

The local news sites and Facebook groups were full of stories about the latest murder. Roman had skimmed them at breakfast time and couldn't bear to read them again. There had been no further developments, and it annoyed him that Phil barely got a mention. The Strangler was the sensation everyone wanted to talk about. His latest victim was little more than a side note.

His mother returned carrying a tray with two massive cappuccino mugs. "They don't have much to choose from here. I've ordered you a ham and cheese panini and a chocolate brownie. They'll bring them over when they are ready."

He thanked her. "I'm really not that hungry."

"Try to eat as much as you can. Please, darling, do it for me." She settled herself in the chair across from him, and he immediately felt the scrutiny of her professional eye.

"Aren't you working today?" he asked, emptying a sachet of brown sugar into his coffee.

"Long weekend off. I'm not back on the ward until tomorrow." She put her elbows on the table, rested her chin on her hands and looked him straight in the eyes. "So, why are you at work? Given the circumstances, surely they'll allow you some time off."

He busied himself stirring the coffee, avoiding her intense stare. "I can't afford to take any time off. They're going to make redundancies at any minute. I can't give them the slightest excuse."

She caught her breath. "Do they know what happened to you?"

"They do."

"And they still made you work today? Any decent employer would have sent you straight home on full pay."

"That's not the way it works. If you're not there, you don't get paid. I'm on a rolling temporary contract. They can terminate it at any time."

"You didn't go to university to work for a bunch of unethical shits. Tell them where to stuff their job. For God's sake, you discovered a body less than twenty-four hours ago. If they can't give you time off for that, they don't deserve to have you."

He sipped the hot coffee. His mother had been in the same job for almost thirty years. She didn't have the first idea about current employment methods or how cutthroat the market was. "I've got to pay my share of the rent. I have responsibilities."

She grimaced. "I'm not sure what you find so appealing about this city. It's a dump. It uses people up and spits them out. You're scraping by in a job you hate. What's the big attraction? Come home, and you won't have to worry about paying rent."

"I won't have a job, either."

"There are plenty of opportunities in the area. There was an accountancy firm in Morpeth advertising for staff just before Christmas. You could be back doing the job you trained for rather than answering phones."

"I don't want to move back to Nyemouth. Not yet. You know small-town life is not for me. I love living in the city. Sure, I have a shitty job, but I'm always on the lookout for something new. I will find it eventually."

"And if you don't?"

"I'll worry about that later. If I don't find another accountancy job by the time I'm thirty, *then* I'll think about leaving."

Her eyes widened in horror. "Thirty? That's four years' time. Your qualifications will be out of date by then."

"I'll do a refresher course if I have to." He heard the irritation in his voice and fought to get it under control. It wasn't her fault, and his mother meant well. "Can we talk about something else? I've got enough on my mind without going through this today."

Their food arrived, giving him a few moments reprieve from her nagging. As the hot panini was put in front of him, Roman realised he was starving. He couldn't remember eating anything after breakfast yesterday, and he'd had no appetite this morning. All he'd had was half a glass of orange juice.

"This looks lovely," he said. "Thanks, Mam." He picked up the panini and took a large bite. The sight of him eating caused his mother to visibly relax, and she started on the tuna sandwich she'd bought for herself.

"It would be nice if you could come home, even if it's just for a few days. Your dad and I worry about you. After you were attacked last year and now this? It's not safe. We'd love to see more of you."

She had tried a different, softer tactic and had succeeded in laying a guilt trip on him. "I've got next Saturday off. I'll see if I can make it home then."

Her face lit up. "Come Friday night. You can get the train after work, and your dad will collect you from the station. He'll love that. And I'll book a restaurant for Saturday. There's a new place just opened in the marina that I've been dying to try. Your brothers will come, too."

Roman had two younger brothers, who, unlike him, had felt no urge to flee the town they grew up in. Both still lived in Nyemouth. Bryce, the youngest, had a house just two streets away from their parents. It should be enough that they were still there, but his mother was determined to bring her eldest back into the fold.

"Don't make any huge plans. I'm not up for it. I just want to come home for a bit of peace. I don't want all your friends pestering me for details on the murder, okay? Saturday night pizza with the family in the house will be enough."

She nodded, smiling. "Of course. I understand, son. Having you home for a few days is enough for me."

Roman knew it wouldn't be. Once in Nyemouth, she would pester him to return more often, show him half a dozen job vacancies and try to tempt him with the allure of coastal living. She probably had a few single hotties lined up to convince him, too. He shouldn't complain. He had a family who cared about him, and after recent events, a couple of days of small-town mundanity would do him good.

* * * *

That night Roman did an hour of unpaid overtime to make up for taking his full lunch break and didn't get home until after seven. It was a relief to find the flat empty. Ashley had left a note to tell him he was going out with Patrick and would spend the night at his place but to call if he needed anything and he would come home. Roman balled up the note and threw it on the bin, relieved that he would not have to endure Patrick that night. He still needed to have the talk with Ashley about boundaries, but maybe he wouldn't have to. The note suggested Ashley had taken the hint to keep Patrick away from him.

Roman was in no mood for company, anyway. He was exhausted. He had little idea of what he'd done at work, having gone through the entire shift on autopilot. If he was questioned about any of it tomorrow, he would not be able to answer. Right now, he didn't care. He just wanted peace, quiet and some time alone.

He scrubbed and pricked a large potato and put it in the air fryer to cook before going to his bedroom to change. The TV was playing in the flat below, but he didn't bother to turn his own on. He didn't have the patience required to watch the news or any of the soaps that cluttered the schedule at this time of night. If Ashley was home, he would be glued to all the usual trash — *Emmerdale, Corrie, EastEnders*. Roman usually managed to tune them out, but for once he wouldn't have to.

After changing into sweatpants and a T-shirt, he went back to the kitchen to decide what he was going to have on his baked potato. He rooted through the fridge and narrowed his options down to tuna and mayonnaise or cheese when his phone rang. He hoped it wasn't his mother calling to make further plans for the weekend.

He glanced at the screen. *Mallon.*

He grabbed the phone and answered. "Hi."

"Hello, handsome, did you miss me?" Mallon murmured in his cool, sexy accent.

It struck Roman as a strange introduction after everything that had happened. "Yeah," he answered without enthusiasm.

"Good. I missed you. I missed your hot ass."

Roman slumped against the counter. For the first time since they'd met, the things Mallon said did not thrill him. "When did you get back?"

"Today. I hoped we could get together tonight. Are you going to come over? You can wear your sexy pants."

Roman stiffened at the lie. "Today? You returned to Blyham *today?*"

"Hey, what's wrong? I thought you'd want to see me. I want to see you."

"Do you have any idea of what has happened?" Roman clenched his jaw. *Is this guy for real?*

"What happened? No...I've been working." A defensive tone crept into his voice.

"The latest murder. Phil Logan, the manager of Julie's. Even you can't have missed it. It's all over the news."

"Oh, well, sure. Yes, of course. You knew him?"

Unbelievable. "You don't know, do you?"

"Know what?"

Roman inhaled and let it out slowly. "Yes, Mallon, I knew him. I was one of the people who found his body."

Now he heard Mallon take a fast breath. "You... *Shit*. Are you all right? Did anything happen to you?"

"Of course I'm all right," he said, suddenly impatient. "I'm alive, aren't I? Phil isn't so fortunate."

"I had no idea. Of course, I read about the murder this morning, but the report didn't give any details. They never mentioned you. I would have called much sooner if I'd known. I'm so sorry, Roman."

"Whatever."

"Why didn't you call me? I could have helped you."

Roman straightened, possessed by anger. "Oh, really? Call you in France? Is that where you were yesterday? Or were you having coffee down on the riverside?"

There was a long beat before he answered. "All right, I'm sorry. You're right. I came back late on Saturday night. I...I should have called, but I needed time. I was working, too, over the weekend. I couldn't have seen you, but if I'd known what you'd been through, I would have been there for you."

"Let me get this right... You got back on Saturday, but you didn't call me until now. We'll overlook the blatant lie you told me earlier. What changed between Saturday and now? I guess you weren't horny then and only remembered to call me when you were lonely and needed a hole to fuck."

"That's not the way I think about you," Mallon said in a rush.

"Isn't it? It certainly feels that way. You're only interested in me when you want to get off. I don't sit around waiting for your booty calls, if that's what you think. I have a life, friends, things to do. I wouldn't have demanded to see you just because you were back, but a text at some point over the weekend would have been nice, instead of having to hear you were back from somebody else."

"Roman, I'm sorry, I should have —"

"Just...just save your breath. I'm exhausted. You know that. This is one drama I can do without. I don't know what you think of me, Mallon. Sometimes I think it's just sex, and other times I feel there's something stronger there."

"There is. I promise there is."

He sighed. "You've got a strange way of showing it."

"Let me prove it to you now."

"No," he said firmly. "Not now. I don't need you now. I don't need you to fuck me to feel better. I need time on my own. I can do this for myself."

"Roman, please. Don't say it's over." There was a genuine note of alarm in Mallon's voice.

"Mallon, I don't know how it can be over when I don't know what this is. I don't know what I mean to you. I don't know if we have anything in common beyond sex. I've got enough on my mind as it is to even think about it now, okay? Just...just leave me alone, and I'll figure things out when I can." Hot tears rolled down his cheeks. "I need to go."

Roman hung up before his voice gave away his emotion. Everything was so damn confusing. Could it get any worse?

He slid onto a chair, put his head and hands on the table and surrendered to the tears.

Chapter Eighteen

"There's something I need to tell you."

The following night, Roman did not work late. He'd had enough of the daily grind, slogging his guts out for a team of unappreciative middle-managers who cared more about targets and metrics than they did about people. He had told his section head about Phil, the trauma of discovering his body and the effect it had on him. She had nodded, uncomfortable and uncertain before telling him he could refer himself to the occupational health department if he wanted to talk about it.

He'd realised in that moment what a terrible company he worked for and that he needed to get out. If they decided to lay him off, they'd be doing him a favour.

The walk home was long, dark and cold but he felt a strange positivity. He'd made a small stand and was no longer prepared to take the shit life threw at him. If it meant giving up his life in the city and returning to the coast, it would not be the end of the world. It could be the start of something new…something better.

As he turned the corner at the top of the street, he saw the lights were on in the apartment. Ashley was home already. Roman hoped he was alone. The mood he was in right now, if he found Patrick spread out on the sofa, he might tell him exactly what he thought of him and throw the fucker out of the door.

As he drew closer, he was aware of someone outside, pacing in front of the steps that led to the entrance.

It was Mallon.

Mallon turned as he approached. He was dressed in jeans and the fur-trimmed flying jacket with a cigarette clamped between his fingers. He dropped the cigarette and ground it out with his shoe, kicking it into the gutter.

"What are you doing here?"

Mallon stepped closer. His eyes were large, glistening pools in the light of the streetlamp. "I had to see you. I didn't want to text or call. I needed to see you for real, to explain."

Roman sighed. Despite the anger that had filled him the night before, he was glad to see him. "How did you even know where to find me?"

"It wasn't hard. You're famous now. It's been driving me crazy, not seeing you. After our call last night, I realised how badly I've handled things. I fucked up, and I'm sorry. I can't begin to tell you how sorry I am."

"I have a lot to deal with at the minute. The smallest thing triggers my anger."

"It's freezing out here. Can we talk inside? Please?"

Roman climbed the steps to the front door. "Follow me."

His heart sank when he entered the flat and heard Ashley and Patrick talking in the living room. *Fuck.* On top of everything else, he didn't need that bastard.

"This way." He led Mallon straight to his bedroom and closed the door behind them.

It was a relief to see he'd made the bed and straightened the place up before leaving for work that morning, not that he could remember doing it. The morning seemed a lifetime ago. He took off his jacket and hung it on the back of the door, gesturing for Mallon to do the same.

"I would show you around, but my flatmates boyfriend is a piece of shit, and I don't have it in me to deal with him right now."

"Why don't you get a place of your own?"

Roman snorted softly. Like his mother, Mallon hadn't a clue how life was for regular working people in the city. "If only it were that easy."

Mallon hung up his jacket. He wore a checked shirt underneath. The red, white and blue colours looked stunning on him. He rummaged in the inside pocket, producing an envelope. "I got you a small present. Just a token to try and make it up to you."

Roman took the envelope and opened it. There were two tickets to the next Blyham FC home match that Saturday.

Mallon looked at him hopefully. "You said you'd like to go but couldn't afford the tickets. I thought we could go together."

He returned the tickets to the envelope and handed them back. Mallon's optimistic smile faded.

"Sorry. I'd love to, but I'm visiting my parents next weekend. I've already committed myself and can't let them down." A dark, sadistic part of him enjoyed the flicker of hurt that passed over Mallon's face. His usual self-confidence, arrogance and ego were absent. For the first time, Roman saw doubt in Mallon's eyes.

"Oh. Okay." Mallon stared at the envelope. "Well, maybe we can go another time, when you are free."

Roman relented. "I'd like that. Just run the date by me first next time."

Mallon nodded and tossed the tickets onto Roman's dresser. "Maybe you know someone who can use these instead. Give them to a friend or colleague."

They stood, looking at one another, the silence lengthening and deepening. Roman didn't know what to say. He'd never been in this situation before. He felt so strongly for Mallon, wanted him more than any man ever, but there was a gulf between them. The last forty-eight hours had made him realise they barely knew each other at all.

"I don't know how to do this," Mallon admitted, letting out an exasperated laugh. "It's all so fucking strange."

This side of him was new. In the time they'd known each other, it was the first glimpse of vulnerability Roman had seen. "What is it that you find so difficult?"

"*Everything*. Don't you realise how hard this is for me? In case you hadn't noticed, I'm not an emotional man — or rather, I'm not the kind of man who shows his emotions."

"Mallon, I don't want to do anything that makes you uncomfortable, but my friend died on Sunday. I found his body. I can't bottle that up and contain it. My emotions, my grief, need an outlet. I need to be with people who understand that, who can help me deal with it. If you can't handle emotions, that's fine, I understand, but you're no good for me right now. It sounds like we both need to deal with our separate issues."

"No," Mallon yelled. "No. That's not it. I don't want to let you go." He stepped closer to Roman. "I want you. I want *us* to be together."

Roman couldn't control himself. He wrapped his hand around the back of Mallon's head and pulled him in for a kiss. Suddenly they were overwhelmed by hunger for each other. They thrust against one another. Roman shoved his tongue into Mallon's mouth — dominating, tasting, breathing him in. Mallon's arms were around him, holding him like the world depended on it, like he never wanted to let go. Roman moaned against Mallon's lips. All his anxiety, his stress, were forgotten for a moment. The kiss reset everything.

"I want you," Mallon said, pulling apart. He unbuckled his belt, unfastened his jeans and turned around. He shoved his jeans to midthigh, then his white underpants, exposing the pale tan line of his arse.

"What are doing?" Roman gasped, breathless with passion.

"I want you to take me," Mallon said, shuffling towards the bed. He leaned forward, presenting his fine arse. "Take my ass. I want you inside me. I want to be the same as you."

Roman didn't question it. The sight of Mallon bent over, exposed, giving up the one thing he had denied him until now was too great. Roman fell to his knees and feasted on the view. Mallon's buttocks were high and pert, the skin several shades paler than the rest of his sun kissed body, lightly covered with silky, dark hair. He planted a hand on each cheek, feeling the muscle, firm but not hard. It was perfection. Roman parted his buttocks and shoved his face inside.

It was what he'd been dreaming of, the day Mallon gave up his arse. Roman devoured it with all his senses, savouring the heat, breathing in the musky scent, tasting the salt on his skin. He moaned and pressed his lips to his hot hole, delighted when he heard Mallon's long sigh of pleasure. Roman teased him with the tip of his tongue, exploring the puckered lines and surfaces of his opening. Roman adored having his own arse eaten and knew exactly what felt good. In seconds, Mallon squirmed and pushed backwards, grinding his hips against Roman's face.

"Yeeeessss," Mallon hissed. "Take it. Take my ass."

Roman attacked with increased vigour. He had wanted to explore this previously off-limits area of Mallon's body for so long. He wanted to drive him crazy with desire, the way Mallon had always done with him. He licked and slurped, getting his tight hole juicy and wet, coaxing it into surrender with each sweep of his tongue.

"Fuck me," Mallon demanded. "I want your cock inside me."

Roman rocked on his haunches. He gave Mallon's arse a gentle smack. "Take off your bottoms."

Mallon did as he'd asked, kicking off his shoes and shucking off his jeans and underwear. Roman retrieved lube from his dresser while Mallon lay face down on the bed, his legs outstretched and parted. Roman hurriedly shed his own clothes until he was down to just his work shirt. He climbed onto the bed. Mallon's beautiful, heart-shaped arse summoned him.

"Are you used to this?" he asked, coating his fingers in lube. He slipped his hand into Mallon's crevice and ran the tip of his finger around his wet hole.

"It's been a while," Mallon admitted.

"How long?"

"Years."

"I'll go easy," Roman said, slipping his finger into the opening. He exhaled as Mallon took him in an incredibly hot, tight grip.

"I just want you to fuck me. Do anything you want to." Mallon pressed the side of his face against the bed and looked over his shoulder at Roman. "Do it."

Roman squirted more lube into his palm and covered his cock from the head to the root, getting it fully slick. No matter how much Mallon begged, if he hadn't been fucked in years, Roman would have to go easy on him. He nudged Mallon's thighs wider and lay over him, taking his weight on one elbow and his knees. He guided his cock to the opening and pushed until he felt the ring of muscle give a little.

"Ready?"

Mallon nodded. "Yes."

Roman lowered himself onto him and eased his cock inside. Mallon was so tight he didn't think he was going to get far. He gave another, more insistent shove and something gave within him. Mallon gasped and stiffened beneath him.

"Okay?"

Mallon drew a series of quick breaths. "Keep going. Fill me."

Roman slipped deeper and deeper, taking his time, attuned to Mallon's body, watching his reactions. Finally, his hips pressed against Mallon's buttocks. Roman shifted his weight, lying down on Mallon's back. He wrapped his arm around his shoulder and rested his head in the crook of his neck. "Tell me when you are used to it."

Mallon rubbed his head against Roman's and gently wriggled his hips from side to side. "Just give me a minute," he sighed. Then he let out a little laugh. "I feel like a virgin again. It must have been even longer than I thought."

Roman kissed him on the cheek and savoured the intense feeling of being inside him. Roman was so used to getting fucked himself, he'd forgotten how pleasurable it was to be on top. Or had it ever been a pleasure until now? Most of the guys he had fucked had been immature, pussy boys. They had laid there, legs wide open, making no effort to connect while he'd fucked them. This was different. Taking Mallon's arse was a life-changing experience for both of them.

"All right," Mallon said, pressing his shoulders to the bed, giving it up. "I'm ready."

Roman eased back and forth, gentle to begin with, noting every reaction from the man beneath him. Mallon pushed his hands forward, above his head. He linked his fingers and sighed. Roman wondered how much he enjoyed it, and how much was a surrender for his benefit after the friction between them. He fucked him long and slow, knowing how exquisite the sensation of a hard cock grazing the sensitive inner lining of his arse could be, gauging where Mallon's prostate lay and ensuring a smooth contact with each inward stroke. Mallon squirmed and widened his legs.

Roman gently nibbled at his shoulder, the base of his neck, and watched as goosebumps rippled across his flesh. Soon he fucked longer and deeper, increasing the pace, confident in Mallon's ability to take it. Mallon grunted with each thrust.

"It this okay?" Roman asked, pushing onto his hands to increase the leverage of his hips.

"Fuck me. Come inside me."

Mallon's words inflamed him. Roman dug his knees into the bed and went harder, faster. Their bodies came together. With every thrust, Mallon pushed his hips backwards, wanting him deeper. The sensations intensified as their emotions strengthened. When Roman couldn't stand the pressure any longer, he increased his pace to a jackrabbit thrust and came. His cock swelled, feeling bigger than ever in the tight confines of Mallon's arse, and the spasms seemed to run through his entire body.

Roman sagged, breathing heavily in Mallon's ear. "Oh my God. *Oh my God.*"

Mallon murmured appreciatively.

"Are you all right?" Roman asked, his heart pounding against Mallon's back.

"Mmm," Mallon wriggled his hips. "But I think you can take it out now."

Roman laughed, withdrawing with care. "Not for you?"

Mallon relaxed. "It…will take some getting used to. I told you, it's been years."

"I appreciate the effort," Roman said, rising from the bed. He grabbed a handful of tissues and wiped his sticky cock.

"It's a good beginning, no? With practice, I can bottom as well as you."

Roman laughed. He pulled on his robe and went to the bathroom to take care of the tissues. His good mood was spoiled within seconds when he heard Ashley and Patrick arguing in the living room.

"I want to watch that," Ashley said, sounding annoyingly passive and whiny.

"Enough of this shit. I'm not watching your fucking soaps all night." There was no humour in Patrick's tone, only anger.

"Give me that back."

"Stop sounding like a cunt."

Mallon was sitting up on the bed when Roman returned. He had put his underpants and checked shirt back on. Roman couldn't blame him. It was cold in the flat now that the heat of passion had died, and he kept the robe on, sitting beside him.

"What's this?" Mallon asked, tipping his heads towards the wall.

"Ashley and Patrick. Charming, aren't they?"

"What are they arguing about?"

"Nothing much. Patrick doesn't need an excuse. He could start an argument in an empty room."

"Asshole."

Roman patted his thigh. "You haven't even met him, and you've nailed it in one."

They shuffled closer, their legs touching. "How long have you lived here?" Mallon asked.

"It will be getting on for two years, I imagine. I like it here. It's well positioned for the city, and Ashley is a great flatmate when he isn't hooked up with awful boyfriends. We've had an occasional bit of abuse from some of the local kids but nothing we can't handle. Homophobia is on the rise all over Blyham. This area is no worse than anywhere else."

"You shouldn't have to put up with it."

"I know. But it's a fact of life. We're still a long way from acceptance."

"Stop acting like a prissy fucking bitch." Patrick's voice boomed through the wall.

Roman sighed. "I can handle abuse outside, in the streets. It's a lot harder to bear when it's our own home."

Mallon sat up straighter. "Do you want me to take care of this asshole?"

"No. God, no. That would only make it worse. Until Ashley wakes up to the fact that he's dating a monster, nothing will change."

Ashley hollered something back at Patrick, but his words were incomprehensible through the walls.

Mallon drew a sharp breath and leapt from the bed. He paced the floor agitatedly. Roman got up to pacify him, concealing his own anger at the other couple.

"Let me put on some music. It will drown them out."

Mallon shook his head. His expression had changed in a matter of seconds, from post-sex bliss to extreme anxiety. Roman had never seen him look so serious.

"We need to talk," Mallon said in a rush. "I didn't come here for sex. There are…things I need to tell you."

Suddenly the floor beneath Roman's feet seemed unsteady, like it would fall away at any time. "Okay." He searched Mallon's features for a clue and got nothing.

"I can't do it here…with them." He jabbed his finger towards the wall. He searched the room for his clothes, picking up his jeans and stepping into them. "I hate this bullshit. There's something I need to tell you, and I can't do it here."

"You're worrying me now."

Mallon found his boots and pulled them on. He avoided Roman's gaze.

The voices from the next room grew louder.

"Let's go," Mallon said, finally looking at Roman. His pale grey eyes were unfathomable. "Please. Get dressed. Let's get out of here. I feel like…the walls are closing in on us."

"I'm not sure I should leave them," Roman said, "when they're fighting."

"Fuck them," Mallon yelled. "They are going to argue whether you are here or not. I need to speak to you, and if I don't tell you tonight, I'm not sure I'll have the courage to ever tell you at all."

The power of his words hung heavily in the room.

"All right," Roman said, unable to stand the strain any longer. There was nothing he could do for Ashley and Patrick, but what he could do for Mallon was listen. "Let's go."

He picked up his clothes and started to dress.

Chapter Nineteen

Confessions

Mallon didn't have a lot to say as they left the flat and walked into town. Roman remained torn. Was it a good idea to leave Ashley and Patrick in the middle of an argument? With his size and strength, Patrick could do some serious damage if the fight turned physical. However, Mallon seemed desperate to talk to him, to unburden himself of some great secret. Was it fair to jeopardise his own relationship for the sake of many long-running disputes between his flatmate and fuck-wit boyfriend?

Roman would text him when they got wherever they were going.

If Ashley gave any indication that he was in trouble, Roman would hurry back.

The night had turned colder in the hour since he'd come home. Their breath swirled in clouds around their faces.

"I'm starving," Roman said. "I only had a yogurt and an apple for lunch today. Can we stop so I can get something hot to eat."

Mallon's brow furrowed in concern. "Shit. I'm sorry. It didn't occur to me, turning up at your apartment, waiting for you to come home. I'm so stupid."

"It's fine…really. It's my own fault for not taking a proper lunch break again."

They came to the outskirts of the city centre. "What do you want? Steak? Pizza? Italian?"

Roman shook his head. They were approaching a small café called Chez Michelle that served food until late. It was basic but reliable, and at this time on a Tuesday night, he figured it would be quiet. They could eat, and Mallon could get off his chest whatever it as that bothered him.

"This will do," he said, pointing across the road to the café. He expected Mallon to complain about the basicness of the establishment or sneer at the name Chez Michelle, but he nodded and followed Roman's lead without complaint. *He's not himself at all.*

There were only five other customers.

"Sit anywhere you like," a cheerful woman in her mid-forties hollered from the bar. "I'll be with you in a minute."

Mallon headed straight for a table in the corner, as far away from the other diners as they could get. Roman took off his jacket and hung it over the back of the chair before sitting. The café hadn't changed much since the last time he'd been here. The walls were covered in faux brickwork wallpaper and cheap prints of the French countryside. The menus were laminated A4 sized pieces of cream card that had seen better days. He didn't care about the posh restaurants Mallon was used to. This was Roman's kind of place, and if Mallon wanted to spend more time with him, he would have to get used to it.

Mallon didn't even look at menu. When the waitress came over, he asked for a large glass of Merlot and nothing else.

"Can I have a beer?" Roman said. "And a burger and fries."

Even the horror of ordering such food in a supposed French café went without comment. Once they were alone, Roman put both hands on the table. "So, what is it you need to tell me?"

Mallon twisted his face. "After you've eaten."

"It's that serious?"

He gave a curt nod in reply.

"You haven't taken off your coat?" Roman remarked.

Mallon seemed to notice for the first time. "I'm cold," he said. "And, I could use a cigarette. Do you mind?"

"Go ahead," Roman said kindly. "I want to text Ashley anyway, make sure he's okay."

Mallon's face was pinched as he stood and headed outside. Roman sent a quick message to his flatmate, telling him where he was and to get in touch if he had any problems. He put down his phone and watched Mallon through the window. He paced the pavement outside the café, drawing on the cigarette. His lips moved, as though he was rehearsing a speech.

Roman couldn't guess what was bothering him so much. Mallon had been the epitome of unflustered cool the whole time he'd known him. Even that first night, when he'd taken down three bullies in a fight, he had been unflappable. What had brought about the change?

Roman watched as he lit another a cigarette.

Something Ashley had said earlier in the week came to his mind. *"What if the Blyham Strangler is actually the French Strangler?"*

Whatever Mallon wanted to tell him, it was deadly serious to him. *Could that be it? Is Ashley right? Is he the killer?*

"Who has been in town at the time of the last two murders that we know of? He has."

Roman dismissed the idea as stupid. Ashley spent too much time watching bad soap operas and fighting with his boyfriend. He thrived on drama. He would suspect Mallon of murder if it made a good story to share with his friends, but there was no basis for it. Whatever was bothering him tonight, it was not that. Roman was certain of it.

The drinks arrived, and by the time Mallon returned to the table, so had Roman's food. The homemade burger looked a lot better than he'd expected it to, accompanied by fresh coleslaw and a vibrant side salad. The fries were deliciously golden.

"Looks good," Mallon said, watching Roman smother the fries in mayonnaise and ketchup while he finally removed his jacket.

"Do you want to share? I can cut the burger in two."

Mallon shook his head. "You need to eat." His voice was stern.

"You sound like my mother," Roman said. He took a large bite. The beef patty was delicious—juicy, perfectly charred and cooked all the way through. So called gourmet burgers served pink in the middle were a particular hate of his.

Mallon sipped his wine. A fleeting grimace passed across his face before he went in for another taste.

It took less than five minutes for Roman to clear his plate. He even ate all the salad. "That was so good. I need to come here more often." He wiped his lips with a serviette then took a swig of beer. "Okay, I'm full. You should be satisfied. Now, are you going to tell me what's bugging you? Surely, it's not our argument from earlier."

Mallon sucked his teeth. "Of course not, that was nothing."

Roman sighed. "Then what is it? I hate secrets. They fester from the inside. Nothing good ever comes from keeping them. Whatever it is, you can tell me."

Mallon's eyes widened and glistened in the low light of the café. He took a breath, shoved his fist in his mouth and bit his knuckle.

"Mallon, please. Just spit it out. I don't know what reaction you expect from me, but I can promise you, it won't be as bad as what you've built up in your head." He moved his hand across the table and brushed his fingers across Mallon's. "Tell me. You'll feel better afterwards."

"I hope you will feel the same." His words were barely above a whisper. Mallon took another breath and reached into his jacket to remove his wallet. He glanced at Roman again, seeming to struggle in his search for words. "There's a reason I return to France as often as I do." He opened the wallet and slid it across the table.

Roman picked it up. There was a small, plastic window inside, the place most people store their driver's licence or ID cards. In Mallon's wallet there was a photograph of two children...a boy and a girl. Roman was terrible at guessing kids' ages, but they looked to be around nine or ten. There was no mistaking who they belonged to. With thick, almost-black hair and startling grey eyes, they were the image of their father.

"This is what you were afraid of telling me? How did you think I would react? You have children. It's not that unusual. I had a boyfriend in the past who was a father, too." He looked at him compassionately. "You go home to see them when you can. I admire you for that."

Mallon chewed his lip, tension still etched across his face. Roman realised this wasn't everything.

Ah. Of course.

"You're still with their mother. Right?"

Mallon couldn't meet his eyes. His lack of reply answered the question.

His aloofness, the curt behaviour when they'd met, suddenly made sense. Roman saw the history of their relationship from a distance, as though having an out-of-body experience. Mallon hadn't been all French and mysterious as Roman had assumed. He was a married man, keeping a secret while he played away in a foreign country. *Jesus.* Roman had slept with married guys in the past, so why had he been unable to read the signs this time? *Because I thought this was different. I thought this was more than just a one-off fuck.*

He closed the wallet and slipped it back towards Mallon, who stared into his wine glass.

"How long have you been married?"

Mallon started to speak but his words choked. He coughed and cleared his throat. "Thirteen years."

Heat crept across Roman's face. Suddenly his head was pounding, and the room closed in around him. "And the children? How old are they?"

Mallon finally raised his eyes. His expression was ghastly. He might be just another man on the make for sex while working away, but he clearly had a hard time with it.

"Carole is eleven," he said. "Mathis is nine." He took a long drink of wine. "It's not what you think."

"That's what all married men say, isn't it? When they've been stringing someone along. '*It's not what you think.*'"

"No." His voice was sharp, drawing attention from the other diners. He leaned forward, lowering his tone. "I'm not like that. Whatever you think of me, it was never that. The reason I'm telling you this now is because…"

"What? You never expected to develop feelings for me?"

Mallon closed his eyes, inhaled through his nose. "That's right. I didn't expect to fall in love with you. That's what makes this so difficult. I don't want to hurt you."

"*I didn't expect to fall in love with you.*" The words took the sting out of Roman's anger. He didn't know how to reply. He'd known there was a powerful connection between them, but he never suspected Mallon's emotions were so deep.

"I love my children," Mallon continued. "I loved their mother once, too. Betrice. But marriage was a mistake…a big one. That is not the fault of the children. They shouldn't suffer for what their parents did. I knew I was bisexual when I met Betrice. It didn't seem so important back then. I thought I could be happy with her, and when the children were born, I was, for a while. Betrice is a complicated woman. She's not a home maker. She likes to socialise — the parties and nightlife, long weekends at beach resorts. She was the first to break our marriage vows. And when I found out she had, it gave me permission to do the same."

Mallon took another drink and composed himself. "As I got older, the attraction I had for other men grew stronger. I still consider myself bisexual, but perhaps the balance has shifted. So, while Betrice had her cocktail party lovers, I began to have men on the side, too. I discovered that other men are willing to engage in uncomplicated sexual liaisons, especially men with similar secrets to keep — no ties, no commitments, just a casual exchange."

Roman's mouth was dry. He licked his lips and took a drink of beer. There was so much to process here. "You have been married thirteen years, unhappily by the sound of it. Why do you stay together if you both want different things?"

"For the children."

"Is that enough? What good can it do them if their parents are so distant."

"They don't know. They won't know for a long time. Betrice is many things, but she is a good mother. We maintain the façade for the sake of Carole and Mathis. We have an understanding that we will preserve the marriage until Mathis is in college."

"That's insane." The words were out of Roman's mouth before he could stop them.

"Insane? Perhaps. Tell me, are your parents together? Are they happy?"

"Yes."

"Then you appreciate the importance of a stable family, of a committed mother and father. I will not let my children grow up without that secure base. It is everything."

Roman was about to reply but killed the words before he spoke. It would do no good to tell Mallon what he said was ridiculous. His marriage was built upon lies — two people living separate lives but pretending to be together for the sake of old-fashioned morality. Children were not stupid. The older they got, the more aware they would become of the gaping chasm between their parents.

If what he's told me is true. Mallon had been lying to him for weeks. How could Roman trust that he was telling the truth now? Mallon was believable. His emotions seemed genuine. *Is that enough?*

"So, are you saying you are going to remain in a loveless marriage for, what, the next eight or nine years?"

He gave a short nod. "We've been married thirteen already. Nine years does not seem too long in the scheme of things."

"Why are you telling me this? You had things worked out pretty neatly — one life in France, another here in Blyham. You had the best of both worlds. What has changed?"

"You. My feelings for you. When I called you last night, I sensed a change. I…I was afraid of losing you, of losing what we have." He shook his head and mumbled something in French. "Shit. I can't explain. I want you to know the truth, and if you decide to be with me, there will be no deception. You'll know everything."

"Be with you. What does that mean?"

Mallon's eyes brightened. "It means anything you want it to." He thumped his chest, right on the heart. "I can honestly say I have never experienced feelings like this for another man. I've always maintained a distance. I rarely saw the same man more than once. If I did, he was always married with secrets of his own to protect. Emotions were never a part of it. *You* made me feel something different." He thumped his heart again. "Something here. Tell me, please. Tell you feel something, too."

Roman struggled to think clearly. The things Mallon said appeared to have come from nowhere. He couldn't remember another time Mallon had mentioned his emotions or viewing Roman as anything more than a sex partner. "Of course, I do," he admitted. "I...I don't even know what this is, but it's all new for me, too. Until I met you, I hadn't slept with the same man more than once for a long time. I can't deny there was something developing between us, even though neither of us acknowledged it."

"Thank God, I am not crazy. I was afraid this was only me."

Roman shook his head. "It's not. I feel it, too." He took a deep breath. "But you have given me a lot of information tonight, and I'm struggling to get my head around it. That you're married with a family is going to take some time to process. And you really picked your moment for it, didn't you? I'm still recovering from the shock of what happened to Phil."

Mallon furrowed his brow. "Shit. I'm a selfish bastard. I didn't even think about that...only myself. I'm sorry, Roman. This confession could have waited. I suppose I panicked."

"It's all right. I appreciate your honesty. If you had told me all this at the beginning, it's unlikely I'd have wanted to see you again. But I'm going to need some time to get my head around it all."

"How long?"

"I can't say. A day or two, maybe?"

Mallon's expression saddened. "Of course. I understand. It's a lot."

"I'm glad I know. So, thank you."

Mallon opened his wallet again and withdrew a plastic card. He passed it across the table.

"What is this?" Roman asked.

"It's the key to my apartment. When you are ready, you can let yourself in at any time."

Roman flushed as another rush of blood went to his head. "Are you sure? This is a big gesture."

"I have already cleared it with the building security team. They know I am giving you this, so you can come and go as you please, even when I'm at work or out of the country. Maybe it will give you a place to escape to if the arguments get too intense at your own apartment."

"I don't know what to say."

"Just take it." Mallon pulled his jacket off the back of the chair. "I've said enough for one night, given you a lot to think about. I'm going to go now. Take your time and think about everything I have told you. There is no rush. I will wait for as long as it takes. And when you reach a decision, you know where to find me."

* * * *

Mallon left Chez Michelle, fastened his jacket to the neck and lit a cigarette. From the other side of the road, a man dressed all in black, with a cap pulled low over his brow, watched, silent and unobserved. Mallon looked like a man with the world on his shoulders. He put down his head and walked along the street, further into the town centre. He had lost the usual arrogant, cock-of-the-walk strut.

Roman remained inside the café, making no attempt to leave himself.

Trouble in paradise?

It would seem so. Whenever these two got together, they could melt ice with the heat they generated. There was none of that tonight. Both looked troubled and lost in their own thoughts.

The man had to make a snap decision. They were clearly doing their own thing this evening. On instinct, he chose to follow Mallon.

He hung back and tracked him from the other side of the road, but the precaution was not necessary. The French man was too absorbed in himself to notice the danger, to suspect he was being followed.

After everything that he'd done, everything he'd achieved, the fear he had generated throughout the city, the man was astonished at how little care these queer men took. They thought they were invincible. Assault and murder were crimes that befell others, never them. He was convinced that not one of his victims had ever imagined it would happen to them until the seconds before he wrung the life out of them.

He recognised the route Mallon was taking. He was cutting through the city centre and down towards the riverfront. The idiot was going to walk home on a dark and cold night.

With a merciless grin, the man shoved his hands in his pockets and followed.

Chapter Twenty

Mallon

Mallon pulled his jacket tight around his neck. He would never get used to the cold in this country. It leached upwards from the ground, penetrating his boots and seeping into his body, first through his toes before spreading its insidious chill through every part of him. He dragged on his cigarette, clutching at the scant warmth it afforded.

What have I done?

Tonight, he might have made the biggest mistake of his life. The wounded look on Roman's handsome face had torn at his heart. Mallon had thought the truth would enable them to move on to the next stage of their relationship, but the pain he had witnessed in Roman's eyes could trigger the exact opposite. He might have lost him.

The notion was unbearable.

Mallon hadn't been ready to play his hand so soon. When he'd returned from France at the weekend, he'd thought the best thing to do was to maintain the status quo. They could continue as they were, seeing each other a couple of times a week. On his most recent trip home, he had missed Roman more than he'd ever thought possible. Betrice had taken the children on a skiing trip two days after he'd arrived, and he'd spent most of the time alone in the house. Previously, he would have enjoyed the peace and privacy. He would have hooked up with one of his fuck-buddies and thought no more of it. Only he had no interest in the local men now. His heart had remained in England, in Blyham, infatuated with the young man who had come into this life just weeks before.

Mallon had realised the strength of his feelings for Roman as he moped around the family home alone. On his return to Blyham, he'd vowed to cool things down between them, to leave a few days before making contact with Roman. It had taken every reserve of strength he had to keep from texting him at the weekend. Mallon had exerted himself with work and at the gym, running. He'd even taken a boxing class at the local leisure centre. None of it worked. No matter what he did, he couldn't get Roman out of his mind. He had eventually submitted on Monday evening and had picked up his phone.

Roman hadn't been as excited to hear from him as he'd expected. He'd been cold and indifferent. When Mallon discovered what Roman had been through the day before, how he'd come into the orbit of the Blyham Strangler, Mallon had panicked. He'd realised then that he might have returned to find there was no Roman at all, and the thought of anything happening to him had filled him with dread.

Despite being married for thirteen years, Mallon had a lot of experience with men, but he had never known emotions as strong as what he had for Roman. He'd never felt like this about anyone before.

He was in love with him…desperate, all-consuming love.

Had he blown it apart by confessing his secret?

Uncertainty chilled him as thoroughly as the cold evening.

Shit! What made him think Roman would understand? Why should he? He was free and single. What cares should he have for the emotional complications of an older, married man?

He'll run. And he'll be right to. He doesn't need your bullshit, you stupid old man.

Mallon stubbed out the cigarette in a waste bin. His hands were too cold to light another. He shoved them deep in his pockets and kept walking. He should have called for a taxi, but some masochistic instinct made him continue. He deserved this discomfort. He quickened his pace. He was already on the downward road to the river. *Not too far now.*

Roman didn't understand what made him stay with Betrice despite the loveless years of their marriage. They did it for the children. Betrice respected that as much as he did. Carole and Mathis would not grow up in the chaos he had suffered as a child. They knew nothing of their parent's troubles and never would. He and Betrice put on a convincing show. They had not had a single wrong word or argument in front of the kids, ever. He intended to keep it that way. He'd made a pact with his wife that they would stay together until the kids were both in college, and Mallon intended to honour it.

His children deserved the very best, and they would have it.

Mallon was born in the resort town of Villefranche-Sur-Mer, the second of four brothers. His parents had run a restaurant on the harbour, working long hours, and the boys were left to care for themselves. When he told people of his childhood, they assumed it had been idyllic. How could it not be? Growing up on the Riviera in a beautiful town, close to Monaco and Monte Carlo.

No one knew the reality, because neither Mallon nor his brothers talked about it. Despite being married and business partners, his parents had an abusive relationship. They were both drinkers and often fought well into the night after they'd finished their shift at the restaurant. His father was a mean-spirited man with a combustible temper. Mallon and his siblings had felt the hard lash of his belt when he was in one of his moods. His temper had a hair-trigger, and it took nothing to set it off.

His mother was only slightly better. She did little to protect her sons from her husband's wrath and wasn't above taking her hand to them herself. Both were guilty of using the boys as weapons against the other during one of their heated fights. One of his worst memories was of being stuck in the middle while they tore at him from either side. He'd thought his arms were going to be ripped from the sockets. He had been eight years old.

He would never allow anything like that to happen to his children. Any parent who would was no parent at all.

When Mallon was fourteen, he had witnessed the death of his best friend Emanuel. The boys had been playing in a cove close to home, swimming offshore and fooling around. The beach had always been his escape. Neither of his parents showed any interest in entertaining their children, and they often left them in the care of neighbours or their friends' parents. Those were the childhood days and memories he truly cherished, until the day he and Emanuel challenged each other to a race. There was a marker a mile from shore, and they bet twenty francs that they could make it there and back before the other. The boys were strong swimmers with no fear of the ocean.

Mallon had reached the marker ahead of his friend and was on the return mile to the beach. His muscles screamed from the exertion, each breath seemed harder than the last to catch, but he would not give in. He had been so immersed in the challenge that he failed to hear the roar of an engine until it was almost upon him. A tourist who had hired a jet-ski had lost control of the vehicle. It had whizzed past Mallon, sending him tumbling in its wake. Despite the screams of the tourist and of horrified observers on a nearby boat, Emanuel was not so lucky. He raised his head and seemed only to notice the ski at the last second. The moment of impact had haunted Mallon for the rest of his life.

That evening, his father had refused to close the restaurant. He had hollered at Mallon about being a reckless shit whose actions had resulted in the death of his best friend. The next morning, oblivious to his tears and the distress he was in, his mother had driven him to school and forced him through the gates. At the height of the summer season, neither parent was prepared to take a day off to comfort their son. It was a kind teacher who took pity and arranged for him to spend the day in the care of his own parents rather than endure the morbid curiosity of his classmates.

Besides the love he felt for his brothers, there were few signs of affection in the family home.

Mallon had been at university, studying in Lyon, when he had received a call from home, from one of the waiters in the restaurant. His mother had stabbed his father eleven times during an argument in the kitchen. Despite the best efforts of the staff and emergency services, they had not been able to save him. His mother had been sentenced to life imprisonment when he was twenty-three years old. Mallon had made his own way in life ever since and had vowed that his children would never experience anything like the disorder and pain of his own upbringing.

His mother had been released from jail the past summer, after serving fourteen years of her sentence. The parole board had deemed she was no risk to the public. Mallon had visited her three time since, in a small village far from where they used to live. He saw little evidence that she had changed. She was mean-mouthed, sullen and ungrateful. She might not pose a danger to members of the public, but there was no way he would ever allow her to meet his children...not ever.

Mallon continued his walk along the Blyham waterfront. Most of the restaurants were busy this evening, their customers huddled inside, out of the cold. *Not much farther to the apartment.* His hands were warm enough to light another cigarette. It was a filthy habit, and he wanted to quit. The children hated it, and though Roman tried not to reveal his distaste, Mallon had noticed the way he turned his head away while he smoked, avoiding the polluted air. Mallon looked after himself in every other way, keeping fit, eating healthily most of the time. Surely he owed it to the people he loved to kick this one remaining vice.

Apart from his children, his life had been an unsatisfying ride for most of the time, as he avoided his parents and had formed a series of unsatisfying relationships.

Roman was the best thing to happen to him in over a decade. He was the perhaps the only meaningful and serious connection he'd made in his adult life.

Mallon couldn't throw that away.

He had no idea how Roman would deal with the bombshell news he'd delivered this evening. It was selfish to expect he would want to, but Mallon would not give up on him easily. He wouldn't take rejection without a fight. Roman cared for him, he was sure of it—maybe not as strongly as Mallon felt for him, but enough to make it work, enough to invest in some kind of future together.

In the beginning it had always been about sex. How could it not be when Roman was the hottest man he'd ever encountered? That face, that body, that ass. *Oh, God, that ass.* Mallon could not get enough of it, especially in those early days. As important as the sexual heat between them remained, something had overtaken it. Mallon looked forward to getting to know Roman. He wanted to take him out, to spend time with him, just to sit beside him and feel his closeness. He loved the deep, rhythmic sound of his breathing while he slept, the gentle murmurs he elicited in his dreams. He adored the sleepy look in his eyes first thing on a morning. Like most younger people, Roman was not at his brightest when he woke up. It only made Mallon love him more.

I can't do without him.

I won't *do without him.*

Mallon reached the outer door of his apartment building. The security guard was not on duty. He let himself into the lobby and bypassed the elevator in favour of the stairs. Despite the lengthy walk back in the cold, he felt a restless energy coursing through his body. He took the stairs two at time, arriving at his apartment door sightly out of breath.

He had left in a hurry earlier, changing out of his suit after work to rush to Roman's place, wanting to get there before he came home. Mallon's cleaning service had been in that day and the apartment was immaculate, though it smelled strongly of air freshener and polish. How different it would be to return here at the end of a busy day to find Roman waiting for him.

Mallon grabbed a tumbler and opened a fresh bottle of Scotch. The whisky was smooth and oaky and soothed his throat as he swallowed. It warmed him from the inside and banished the cold of the January evening. He drained the glass and poured another.

He crossed to the window, unlocked and opened the sliding door onto the large balcony. He stepped out and gazed over the side, half hoping he would see Roman making his way along the waterfront towards him, that he would have wasted no time following him from the café.

The pavements were empty.

Mallon deflated further. *Of course he isn't there*. He wondered again whether he had made a terrible mistake? He couldn't stop wondering what was going through Roman's mind. Would he eventually accept the secrets Mallon had revealed? Or was it over between them for good?

He questioned if he should text? Nothing serious. He could keep it casual. Let Roman know he had made it home safely and ask if he'd done the same. *No, don't make things worse than they already are. You've already overloaded the poor boy. Give him space and let him get in touch with you.*

The wait would be interminable.

Better to wait than fuck it up for good.

Mallon stood on the balcony, gazing at the inky black water of the river and finished the whisky. He loathed this feeling of utter helplessness. With a sigh, he wandered back inside, leaving the door open a few inches to air out the smell from the cleaning products. He refreshed his glass for the third time and went into the bedroom, checking his phone. There were no messages. Resisting the urge to call, he put down the phone and undressed. It had been a long day. He'd gone into the office at six that morning to ensure he got away in good time. He would take a shower, have something light to eat and try to get an early night. It was wishful thinking. He knew it would be impossible to sleep until he had heard from Roman.

He ran the shower as hot as he could take it and stood under the faucet. He shampooed his hair and lathered his body, washing away the sweat and oils of the day and a little of the stress, though he suspected the whisky had done more to relax him than the water. After ten minutes beneath the scorching jets, he turned it off and stepped out. His body tingled with the heat.

He grabbed a towel from the rail and dried himself from head to toe, enjoying the softness and freshly laundered scent of the towel.

It had done him good. He felt better than when he'd gone into the shower. With another whisky and some food inside him, maybe he could unwind enough to sleep that night.

The bathroom resembled a sauna with its swirling wraiths of steam.

Mallon wrapped the towel around his waist and opened the door to the bedroom.

As he stepped towards the bed, lost in his thoughts of Roman, he became aware of a change in the atmosphere.

Mallon realised he was not alone a fraction too late.

A blow to the back of the head with a heavy object sent him sprawling to the floor, and his entire world spun in a cruel vortex.

And after that...darkness.

Chapter Twenty-One

An Unexpected Encounter

Roman remained at the table for a long time after Mallon had left, staring at the debris on his plate, his mind somewhere far away. All the things Mallon had told him tumbled through his head in an un-sequenced scramble. His marriage and children were the least surprising. Mallon had provided nothing but the barest scraps of information about his life in France until now. Roman hadn't given it a huge amount of thought, but it made perfect sense that he'd had something to hide.

Roman had tried to steer clear of married men, especially the ones who were married to women, for the longest time. They were everywhere of course, on Grindr and other dating apps, even at The Viaduct, but he had developed a good instinct for spotting them. A few were honest enough to admit the fact straight up, asking for complete discretion in their initial contacts. Whenever it happened, he gave a polite rejection and blocked them from contacting him again.

Roman had old-fashioned values about marriage. He was fine with open relationships and couples who liked to pick up a third party for a threesome, when everything they did was consensual and honest. It was the guys who cheated and played around on the side that he had the issue with.

The wives and partners of those men were not party to the arrangement. They waited at home, believing their stories of working late or drinks with the boys while their husbands took dicks in the vaults of The Viaduct or hooked up with some cutie they had met through an app.

Roman had always believed people could do whatever they wanted to while they were single, could fuck as many random strangers as they desired, but once they made a commitment to another person, they should honour it.

He didn't have many rules in life, but avoiding married men was one of them.

There were always a few who slipped through. Some men were so practised at lying and deception, it was impossible to figure them out until it was too late. He'd had a thing with a nice guy called Paul about a year before. They had gotten together three or four times and had great chemistry, Roman had thought they had the potential to take things further. When he'd invited Paul to watch a mid-week game of football, he'd admitted he couldn't. It was his husband's birthday, and they were going to dinner. When Roman asked if they had an open relationship, Paul had to admit that they didn't. His screwing around was entirely one-sided.

Though Roman had seen him around The Viaduct a few times since then, he'd given Paul a wide berth.

Married men always found a way to justify what they did. *My wife doesn't understand me. She doesn't like sex anymore. No one understands bisexuality. This is the only way I can be my true self.* Mallon wasn't the first guy to tell him that he stayed in an unhappy marriage for the sake of his children.

Roman had managed to negotiate a simple and clean path, avoiding the pitfalls of horny husbands and their shitty excuses.

Until now…until Mallon.

The waitress returned to clear the table, breaking the spell of introspection.

"Can I bring you anything else?" she asked. "Dessert? Coffee?"

Roman was about to say he'd have the bill then changed his mind. "Can I have a double vodka with just the tiniest dash of Coke?"

"No problem," she said with a jovial smile. "I'll bring that right over."

He checked his phone. There was a text from Ashley to say everything was fine with Patrick. *Another one with his head up his own arse.* He would stand by that lie for as long as he had to. Roman didn't bother to reply. He had enough issues of his own to think about.

The waitress delivered the vodka, and he took a long, gratifying drink.

What now?

The obvious answer was to tell Mallon they were finished. They had no ties to each other. Mallon could piss off back to France and unpick the complicated web of his personal life—or stay here and find another fuckboy to satisfy his needs. There was no reason they ever had to see each other again.

Apart from one.

Mallon had said he was in love with Roman, and though Roman had avoided entertaining even the idea of love for Mallon in case it should end in disaster, he couldn't deny he felt the same. He thought it was just

215

sex, that he was infatuated with him and his beautiful cock, but the way he thirsted for him on the nights they weren't together, how much he missed him when he returned to France, proved his feelings ran far deeper than anything physical.

Mallon's confession had come as an even bigger shock than the news of his wife and kids.

Since they'd gotten together, Mallon had kept a tight lid on his inner self. Roman knew he liked good quality food and drink and loathed junk, but other than those things and sex, he had not expressed a great passion for anything. Roman knew Mallon was obsessed with his arse but had no clue if he was interested in anything else about him. He didn't even know what kind of music he liked or what TV shows he was into. Mallon's life seemed to revolve around two things—work and fucking.

And now he says he's in love with me.

Roman took another good drink of vodka.

He picked up the key to Mallon's apartment and turned it over in his hands. What was the significance of this? It was a bold step to offer an open invitation to his home. Until now, Mallon had given no indication he wanted Roman to be a more significant part of his life in Blyham.

It was a lot to take in. The family issues would have to wait. Right now he needed to get his head around his own feelings, what he felt for this sexy, fascinating and infuriating French man who had gotten under his skin.

He blew out a long breath. His intention had been to go straight home. He needed time to think and get his thoughts in order, but that seemed impossible. There were too many unanswered questions that would keep him up for the rest of the night. There would be no opportunity to talk things through with Ashley, either, not with Patrick lurking around the flat. Roman could do with his friend right now, but Ashley had made it clear that Patrick was his priority.

Fuck it. He couldn't let this lie. He needed to talk to Mallon again...tonight.

Roman asked for the bill and ordered an Uber. He would have enjoyed the walk from here to the riverside, but after what had happened to Phil, he knew better than to risk it. The Blyham Strangler worked on a cycle. It would be unlikely for him to strike again so soon, but there were other dangers on these streets. It would be just his luck to encounter a homophobic gang between here and the apartment. An Uber was the most sensible option.

The car arrived within five minutes. Roman's heart raced as they drove through the city streets. He sent a quick text to let Mallon know he was on his way. Though Mallon had given him permission to come and go as he pleased, it seemed wrong to let himself in unannounced.

What if Mallon regretted giving him the key already? He could have changed his mind about everything by the time Roman saw him. No matter how complicated this was for Roman, it had to be a hundred times worse for Mallon. And what kind of future could they have? Mallon had already made it clear he would not divorce his wife until the youngest child was in university.

Roman sighed. The questions would not quit. They spun around his head, out of control, and he couldn't see clearly.

Do I really want to get involved with this? To be the part-time lover of a family man from France?

There would always be a huge part of Mallon's life he would never experience or understand. At twenty-six, did he want to spend the next eight or nine years waiting for a divorce that might never happen? He only had Mallon's word that his marriage was on the rocks. What if it was just a fanciful story to string him along and keep sex on tap here in Blyham?

When the car arrived at the riverside, Roman was tempted to tell the driver he had changed his mind and to take him home instead. The temptation was strong. Maybe this decision would be easier in the morning. He wasn't committing to spending the night here. He'd only come to hear what Mallon had to say. He could call another driver and leave whenever he wanted to.

Roman stepped out.

The night was even colder here than in the city centre. A chill wind from the North Sea blew down the river and cut through to his bones.

He looked up at the building and saw the lights were on in Mallon's apartment. He shivered, filled with apprehension, and wrapped his fingers around the key card in his pocket.

As he moved towards the front door, a figure stepped out of the shadows to his left.

"Hey. Fancy seeing you here," the man said.

He was dressed in a thick leather jacket with a woollen hat and gloves. There was something familiar about the light Birmingham accent and the thick-set frame.

"Sorry," Roman said. "Do I know you?"

The man gave a snort of amusement and tugged off the hat, revealing a mussed-up crop of blond hair. "I really don't make much of an impression on you, do I?"

In the lamplight, Roman recognised the handsome, square-jawed face. "Oh, Will, hi." For a one-time encounter from a year ago, he had run into him a lot lately.

"Ah, then you remember my name this time."

Roman guessed it was meant to sound light-hearted and funny but there was a patronising sound to Will's words.

He shrugged. "I didn't recognise you in the dark, that's all. What are you doing here? Is this where you live?"

Will moved nearer to him. "Nope. Came down this way for a hook-up, that's all. Was hardly worth the effort, if you know what I mean."

Roman forced a laugh. Will stood between him and the entrance, showing no sign of stepping aside. "I think we all know what that's like," he said, humouring him but wishing he would go away.

Will's eyes narrowed and he looked Roman up and down. "Maybe the night is not a dead waste after all." He came closer. "How about we go pick up where we left off last summer? You have a beautiful body. I'd love to get into it again."

Roman pulled back. *This is just weird.* He laughed nervously. "I'm flattered, really. But I'm seeing someone." He gestured to the building. "He's waiting for me now, so I should get inside. It's too cold to stand around talking out here, right?"

Will still didn't get out of his way. He stared directly into Roman's eyes. "Oh, that's right. Frenchy. You're fucking the moody French guy, aren't you?"

"His name is Mallon," Roman said, no longer trying to humour him. Will was behaving like a total creep. Whoever he'd come here to see had probably blown him out for the same reason Roman had last year. There was just something off about him. "How do you know who I'm seeing, anyway?"

Will laughed. "It's a small city, small scene. Everybody knows who everyone else is fucking, don't they?" He stepped nearer. "How about I come up with you, and you can introduce us? The French invented the ménage à trois."

Roman had heard enough — Patrick and Ashley and now Will. What had gotten into everyone tonight? They were acting like there was a full moon. "It was nice running into you." He stepped around him and headed for the door, the key already in his hand. "Take care."

"What's that Frenchy got that I haven't, anyway?" Will hollered after him.

Roman's pulse quickened. He suddenly felt very uncomfortable. He swiped the card and was grateful to see the security light turn from red to green. He hurried inside and ensured it locked behind him.

Will stood about ten yards away, watching and grinning.

What a creep. To think I once fancied him.

Roman turned and crossed the floor to the elevator. When he glanced back to the door, Will had disappeared.

Unnerved by the bizarre encounter, Roman pressed the switch to summon the lift.

Chapter Twenty-Two

Facing a Killer

The door to Mallon's apartment was closed. Roman wondered whether he had seen the text announcing his arrival? What should he do? Did he knock or go ahead and let himself in? It didn't feel right to waltz straight in for the first time without an invitation.

He knocked and waited.

No answer. He knocked again.

Maybe Mallon was asleep or taking a shower or a phone call.

When his third attempt went unanswered, Roman swiped the card and opened the door.

The apartment was silent. No music or TV. No sound from the bathroom or kitchen.

"Hello," he called out. "Mallon, it's me. Are you here?"

Roman closed the door behind him and walked into the living room. He froze.

Mallon was sprawled half across the sofa, his lower body trailing on the floor. He was naked and motionless. Then Roman saw the blood. It was streaked across his back, down his buttocks and his legs. Mallon's ankles and wrists were fastened together with black plastic strips that looked like cable ties.

He experienced an awful sense of déjà vu...of finding Phil.

No. Not again.

Roman rushed forward. He put his hand on Mallon's rib cage and after a moment detected the faint rise and fall of his breath. His face was buried in a cushion.

"Mallon," he said gently, easing his head up. His eyes were closed and swollen. There was more blood around his nose, and he was gagged with a pair of socks, knotted together. Roman gently eased the gag away from his mouth, making it easier for him to breath.

Mallon let out a low moan.

Thank God, he's alive.

Roman rushed to the kitchen, hauling open drawers until he found a pair of scissors. He raced back to Mallon's side and snipped the ties at his wrists and ankles. Mallon moaned again, louder this time and began to rouse. Roman slipped his elbows beneath his armpits and hauled him upwards and over, getting him into a supported sitting position.

Mallon looked like he'd taken a beating to the head and torso. Roman cast his eyes around the room. The place looked the same as always. He could see no sign of any robbery.

Could whoever had done this still be here?

Roman eased Mallon into a comfortable position on the sofa. He hurried back to the kitchen. After all that had happened in the city recently, he couldn't afford to take any chances. He opened a drawer and took out a lethal-looking steak knife. Roman doubted he would have the metal to use it on anyone, but holding it gave him a sliver of confidence.

He was familiar with the layout of the apartment and moved cautiously around the living room, checking behind the curtains. The balcony area was clear. He moved on to check the bedroom and bathroom. No sign of any disturbance.

If Mallon's attacker was still here, the only place they could hide was inside the walk-in closet. The doors were shut. Roman's heart was in his throat. *Get out*, a voice inside warned. *Get the fuck out and call the police*. If the culprit was still here, he couldn't leave Mallon alone in the apartment with them.

The closet doors were mirrored. If there was anyone on the other side, they wouldn't be able to see out. Roman crept forward, keeping his step light. Surprise was the only advantage he had. Moving close to the door, he inched his free hand to the opening and raised the knife to his shoulder, ready to attack. His heart beat so loudly that whoever was in there must surely hear it.

He took a deep breath and hauled the door wide.

Empty.

There was the dresser, the rails of clothing.

He dipped low, checking the floor for any tell-tail legs and feet that would give away anyone hiding within the rails. There was no one.

Roman released his breath.

Whoever had attacked Mallon was not here now.

He rushed back to the living room. Mallon was sitting up straighter. His eyes fluttered.

"Roman," he croaked.

"Don't try to speak. I'll get something for the blood."

He raced to the bathroom, returning with a pile of towels.

"Let me check you over," he said. "I need to stop this bleeding."

"It's just my nose," Mallon said. "I took a beating. Bruises…nothing worse."

"It looks a hell of a lot worse than that."

Mallon winced as he gently dabbed a towel around his face.

"Bastard…jumped me from behind."

Roman cautiously wiped the blood from Mallon's torso and groin area, searching for any puncture wounds or lacerations. It was a relief to find none. "Who did it?"

"I've never seen him before." Mallon flexed his fingers and wrists, getting the circulation going after the restriction.

"Was he waiting for you when you got home? I can't see any sign of a break in, and it doesn't look like anything has been taken, either. I'm going to call the police. You need an ambulance, too. We don't know what kind of damage he could have done beneath the skin."

"I'll do some fucking damage if I see the bastard again."

"That's a problem for another time."

"Clothes. Can you get me something to put on before you call anyone. I had just stepped out of the shower when he jumped me. There are jogging bottoms in the second drawer of the dresser."

Roman watched him carefully. There didn't appear to be any sign of confusion or concussion, at least not for now. He knew there could be a delay between injury and symptoms showing. Mallon needed to be checked out by a doctor. Satisfied that he was all right for the moment, he returned to the bedroom to fetch the jogging bottoms and a hoodie.

He eased the bottoms over Mallon's feet and up to the knees before helping him to stand and pulling them all the way.

Mallon groaned in pain.

"Sit back down," Roman told him.

"No, it's easier if I stand." He shuffled around until he could support himself against the back of the sofa.

Roman gave him a hand to get the hoodie on and fasten it. Mallon grimaced as he flexed his shoulders.

"Did you get a look at who did this?"

"Damn right. The bastard will wish he'd never been born when I see him again."

"What did he look like?"

"Well-built and strong. He used his weight to his advantage. If he hadn't taken me by surprise, it would not have made a difference. He hit me over the head and pinned me down while I was still out of it."

Roman trembled. The adrenaline was wearing off. "He could have killed you. What else."

"Early thirties, maybe. Blond. Dressed in black."

Roman froze. *Shit. No. It couldn't be.*

And the words he'd heard less than ten minutes earlier came crashing back. *"What's that Frenchy got that I haven't?"*

"Oh, my God, Mallon. I think I know who did this to you." His mind was already whirling backwards, to when he'd first met Will, trying to remember how many times he had encountered him since. It seemed like Will had always been there, lurking on the outskirts of the village, making himself known only when it suited him. *Is Will the Blyham Strangler? Surely not.* This attack on Mallon didn't fit the strangler's pattern. He would never have left him alive.

"Who is he?"

"To be honest, I'm not even sure. His name is Will. I don't know his surname. I hooked up him with last year, before I ever met you. It was nothing. Really, less than nothing. But I saw him tonight, before I came in. He was outside the building. He's beefy, well-built with short, dark-blond hair, exactly as you describe."

Mallon gripped the back of the sofa. He swayed a little and a woozy, vacant look came over his face. He snapped into focus a second later. "Then it shouldn't take the cops long to find him. Call them."

"I'm getting you an ambulance first. The police can wait."

Roman took out his phone and used his fingerprint to open the screen lock. He saw, a fraction of a second too late, movement over Mallon's shoulder. A figure, dressed completely in black, slipped from behind the curtains at the French windows, and with three assured steps, came up behind Mallon and placed the jagged blade of a hunting knife at his throat.

"Isn't this cute," Will said.

Roman hadn't realised when he saw him outside that he was dressed in dark commando gear – a black jacket, the woollen hat, black leather gloves. He even had some kind of rucksack fastened on his back. His blue eyes glistening with dark delight. He must have climbed onto the balcony from the street and gained access through the sliding doors. In that moment, Roman had no doubt that Will was the Strangler.

Mallon gritted his teeth. Will had an arm around his chest, the lethal blade pressed to his throat. Roman saw the workings of Mallon's mind, as he tried to weigh up his options, his chances of disarming Will. Under difference circumstances, he could have done it. Will couldn't know what a skilled fighter he was. But Mallon had taken a beating and was likely concussed.

One wrong twitch of a muscle and Will could draw that knife and slice his neck wide open.

Roman looked Mallon in the eyes and shook his head, praying he wouldn't attempt any heroics.

"Wise move," Will jeered. "You should take notice of what your boyfriend tells you. He's probably thinking he can sweet talk me out of killing the pair of you. What do you say? Think we should give him a chance?" He tightened the arm around Mallon's chest. "I'd hate for either of you to think I'm unreasonable."

Fuck. He's mad. It was obvious in the wide roll of his eyes, in the whites that now showed clear all around the iris. *Why didn't I notice this before?* Will had seemed a little needy and desperate, but Roman had never taken him for an all-out psycho.

"You killed Phil last weekend?" Roman said, his voice hard with anger.

Will's lips spread into a joyous grin. "Well done. You've figured it out faster than I expected."

"Why?"

"If I knew the answer to that, I could stop myself. But I have no idea. These men present themselves to me and something clicks in my head, sealing their fate." He pressed the blade closer to Mallon's neck. A thin trail of blood trickled onto his collarbone. "Only you two are different. You might have noticed that."

It was only three days since he had killed Phil. The Strangler usually worked on a two-to-three-month cycle. "Why us?"

Will snorted. "That's another question I wish I had the answer to. But the truth is I'm as bewildered as you are." He put his mouth closer to Mallon's ear. "Don't go thinking you're anything special, Frenchy? Quite the opposite. If you weren't hooking up with fuckboy here, you wouldn't have come to my attention. You're not my type." He gave a cold laugh.

Round the fucking bend. As Will babbled, Roman hurriedly ran through their options. If Mallon's apartment was wired into any security system or panic button, he hadn't let Roman in on it. And he'd already put down the steak knife and scissors, which were both far out of reach, not that he would feel equipped to use them. There was something in Will's stance, in the way he restrained Mallon and held his knife, that suggested military training. He could cut Mallon's throat and bury the blade in Roman before he ever reached those discarded weapons.

He thought about the attack spray they had issued to customers at Julie's. Where was it? He'd been carrying it around for weeks. *Damn.* It was in another jacket.

It was hopeless. Roman didn't have a clue how to fight back. His only chance was to keep the madman talking.

"I didn't realise you were so into me," he said, attempting to hide his fear and keep his tone soft. He looked Will straight in the eyes. "I thought you didn't like me that much."

"Bullshit. You knew. You thought you were too good for me...just a hot little fucker who could have any man he wanted. I wasn't offended. The truth is I planned to kill you last October." He snorted again. "Not sure what changed my mind about that. I liked keeping tabs on you, watching what you were up to, saving you for a later date."

Mallon sneered something in French.

"What's that, arsehole?" Will snarled in his ear. "*Speak English, for fuck's sake.*"

"I said you're a madman," Mallon growled.

Will's features softened. "Mad? No, I'm not mad. A madman would have been caught by now. After all this time, the police still don't have a clue who I am. Could a madman do that? Be so cunning and so patient? I don't think so."

Roman saw a thread of hope in Will's vanity and grabbed it. "You have been clever. Really clever, to get away with it for so long."

"And I'll keep getting away with it. Tonight, you two? This is the biggest risk I've taken. I can't hang around a shitty city like this and hope to avoid attention. After tonight, I'll be gone, a shadow that fades with the morning. Then, when I'm ready, when the time is right, I'll begin again in a new place...Manchester or Liverpool. Let's face it. There's no shortage of horny queers wandering aimlessly into danger for the sake of a dick." He gave a short, self-satisfied laugh.

Mallon must have sensed a change in Will. His eyes flashed at Roman, full of determination. Whether Will had relaxed his hold as he revelled in his deadly achievements or became distracted, Mallon seemingly seized the opportunity and delivered a sharp, backwards jab with his fist. From the pitch of Will's shriek, Roman knew he'd delivered the blow straight to his balls. As the knife moved clear of this throat, Mallon ducked and spun. He came at Will full on, his hands raised for a martial arts strike, but Will was too fast. He lashed at Mallon with the knife, slashing him across the chest, tearing the hoodie. Roman saw a streak of blood as Mallon tumbled across the sofa.

Will raised the knife, ready to plunge it into Mallon's back.

"No," Roman yelled, racing forward.

Will turned on him, the knife raised. His face was contorted into an ugly mask of rage. "It's about time I stuck it to you." He lunged towards him.

Roman flew to the side. A rush of air passed his face as the blade missed him by centimetres. Will grabbed his jacket with his free hand, pulling him in.

"Come here, you little cunt."

His grip wasn't strong enough, and Roman elbowed him aside, scrambling around the coffee table. He heard the rasping rage in Will's breath. The killer was right behind him.

Roman's shin struck the corner of the coffee table. Pain lanced through his leg. He ignored it and rushed on. *The steak knife. Where the fuck did I leave the steak knife?*

His mind flashed through his options in milliseconds. If he could make it to the bathroom, he could lock the door. His phone was in his pocket, and he could hold Will back in time to call the police. But that would leave Mallon at his mercy. Will could fulfil his twisted wish and claim at least another victim before making a run. There were more knives in the kitchen drawer, but Will would be on top of him before he even got one open.

Will snatched the neck of his coat, hauling Roman towards him.

Shit, this is it. The blade would be in his back in a second.

Reacting instinctively, Roman let his body go limp. A dead weight, he dropped to the floor and Will lost his grip on him again.

Then he saw the steak knife. It had fallen to the left of the sofa. Roman scrabbled towards it. It was hopeless. Will's heavy step was right behind him. A powerful kick delivered to the ribs sent Roman sprawling. It unbalanced him more than it hurt.

Undeterred, he clambered towards the knife. This was the bastard who had murdered his friend, who had taken all those innocent lives. Roman would not become his victim without a fight.

Will was above him, his feet planted on either side of his body.

Roman snatched at the knife handle. He twisted and rolled. He had a split-second sight of Will bending towards him with the jagged blade. With a scream of rage, Roman thrust the steak knife into Will's upper thigh. All squeamishness was gone. He thumped his free hand on top of the other, forcing the blade deep. It tore through flesh and scraped bone.

Will roared and staggered backwards, dropping his own weapon. His teeth were bared as he gazed in shock at the handle that stuck out of his thigh. He eyes flickered towards Roman, burning with anger and hate.

"I'm gonna gut you like a fish."

Roman didn't waste his advantage and booted Will in the shin with all the force he had. Will fell backwards. He caught the coffee table with the back of his knees and tumbled over it. As he flailed on the floor like an animal, Roman spotted Will's hunting knife and snatched it. He staggered to his feet.

Will was already recovering and rising. As he realised Roman had his weapon, he gripped the handle of the steak knife and hauled it out of his leg. He snarled at the pain but seemed impervious to it.

They glared at each other, the coffee table separating them.

On the sofa, Mallon rose to a sitting position.

Will spotted the easier target and moved towards him, but Roman was quicker. He got between them, thrust the hunting knife at their attacker. Any misgivings he had about using a knife were forgotten. If this was to be a battle to the death, he would fight.

"Is this what you want, you bastard?" he lunged at Will, who backed away. Despite the dark colour of his clothes, Roman saw that the entire right leg of his trousers was wet with blood.

Will stared at him with pure hatred. Then his eyes darted between Roman and Mallon.

A loud knock at the door startled all of them.

"Mr Garnier," a male voice yelled. "We've had a report of a disturbance. Please open the door."

Thank Christ. Their fight had been heard.

"You're finished," Roman said to Will, then louder so the man on the other side of the door could hear. "Call the police."

"It's over for now," Will snarled. "But I'll be back to finish you another time."

Despite his injured leg, he ran for the sliding doors and out onto the balcony. With incredible agility, he went over the side. Roman rushed after him and watched as he clambered as far down as he could from the first-floor apartment, then let go, dropping and rolling when he reached the ground. He staggered to his feet and gave one last murderous look at Roman before limping along the waterfront.

"The bastard isn't getting away."

Roman turned, shocked to hear Mallon's voice behind him. Before he could stop him, Mallon swung his legs over the balcony and scrambled down exactly like Will had done. He dropped to the ground and rolled in the same expert way.

Roman yelled at him to stop, but it was no good.

Mallon chased their attacker along the riverside.

Chapter Twenty-Three

A Killer Escapes

Although it was only on the first floor, the drop to the street below was too much for Roman. He lacked the physicality of the other two men and didn't like heights. He scrambled back into the apartment and bolted for the door.

A security guard and two neighbours were standing in the hall.

"What's going on?" the guard asked.

Roman pushed past him, heading for the stairs. "They've gone over the balcony," he shouted. "We need police and ambulance. Tell them it's the Blyham Strangler. He's down on the waterfront heading towards the town."

"The Blyham Strangler?"

Roman didn't hang around to the explain. He'd lost enough time already. He leapt down the stairs, two and three at a time. His heart hammered against his chest. He was breathing so hard and fast it hurt the back of his throat.

What was Mallon thinking? Going after him. He was wounded, more than likely concussed. Climbing over balconies in pursuit of a serial killer was crazy. But Will was injured, too. He couldn't get far if the cops arrived fast.

Roman reached the bottom, sprinted across the lobby and out through the main doors. He turned immediately right and saw the two figures about three hundred yards ahead. He pummelled onwards, fuelled by adrenaline.

Did Will still have the steak knife? He couldn't remember what had happened to it after their fight. Mallon was completely unarmed. And in his wounded state, his martial arts skills might be useless.

Roman raced on, gaining on the two men. Their injuries were slowing them down. As he got closer, he saw that Mallon had gained ground and was almost on top of Will.

Why is there no one else to help?

They were in front of the riverside developments, a stretch of bars and restaurants. Roman glanced to his right, hoping someone might notice.

"Help," he yelled, his throat raw with the effort. "Help."

It worked. Several faces appeared at the window of one of the restaurants.

He repeated his call for help. "The Blyham Strangler," he bellowed.

Ahead of him, Mallon put on a sudden burst of speed and, with a leap, was upon Will. He latched onto his back. They were still a hundred yards ahead of Roman. Mallon had his arms and legs wrapped around the killer, using his weight to restrain him. Roman pounded the pavement. If he could reach them, he and

Mallon should be able to hold Will until the police arrived.

The two men struggled. Will twisted from side to side, trying to dislodge the weight on his back. Roman glimpsed a flash of steel. *He still has the knife.* Tapping undiscovered reserves of energy, Roman ran faster. His could no longer feel his legs, was just a blur of motion, propelled by fear and desperation.

The fight had drawn more attention from the waterfront businesses. A group of people rushed across the terrace of one of the pubs, making their way towards the fight.

Will staggered, weaving back and forth, unbalanced by Mallon, who clung resolutely to his back.

Thirty yards. Then twenty. Roman would reach them before the people from the pub.

The two men wavered, precariously close to the edge of the quay. Ten yards. Roman was almost there. He reached out his arms, ready to wrestle Will to the floor. Just as he was about to grasp Will's jacket, he staggered backwards.

Mallon and Will topped over the edge of the quay. Roman's heart fell a fraction of a second before he heard the splash.

"Nooooooo."

The river was black, save for the illumination of the buildings on either side. Roman scanned the surface. Apart from the disturbance of where they had gone in, he saw nothing.

"Mallon," he screamed.

Nothing. Neither of them resurfaced.

There were voices behind him.

"The current will take them down," someone said.

Then a head broke the surface, ten yards on and drifting downriver. He recognised the black woollen hat. It was Will.

Then another head appeared farther out, choking on the water.

Roman reacted on instinct, diving straight into the river.

The shock of the cold made him draw an involuntary breath. He burst for the surface, coughing. He was alive. He still had feeling. He struck out in the direction he'd last seen Mallon. Frantic voices yelled at him from the riverside. He powered on. The river drew him downstream. He'd heard about the currents before but had no idea they were this strong.

Mallon was weak, injured. Roman knew he had to find him before the river took him. He crawled through the cold, black water. It would not end like this.

He paused, lifting his head.

"Mallon," he yelled into the night.

"H-here…"

Roman lowered his face into the water and sped in the direction of the voice.

Can't lose him. Won't *lose him.*

Every stroke was more leaden and laborious than the last.

He paused again, searching.

There was a figure in the water, just ahead of him. *Mallon. Thank God.*

With another surge, he made it.

Mallon's face was ghastly in the lights from the riverside. His skin was as ashen as a corpse. There was barely any animation in his features. If he stayed in the water much longer, he would be finished.

"I've got you," Roman said. His own teeth chattered as he spoke. He swam behind Mallon, slipping his arms beneath his shoulders and easing him onto his back. He would need strength for both of them on the return journey. Roman kicked for the bank. His body seemed independent of his brain, doing everything it could to keep the two of them alive. The currents dragged at their limbs, trying to take them down, but he kept on pushing, fighting against it.

We're not going to die like this. Not tonight.

The voices from the bank were nearer, louder. Roman adjusted course, moving in their direction. Mallon was a dead weight in his arms. *Please let him be breathing.* There was nothing Roman could do to help him until they reached land. Each kick required more effort than the last, and he could no longer feel his legs for the cold.

He twisted his neck to check their progress. A crowd of people beckoned to him. *Almost there. Keep kicking. Keep moving.*

His head bumped against the wall of the quay. They had made it. Hands reached for him. Roman turned in the water, pushing Mallon towards their rescuers.

"Take him first."

They were blessed that the tide was in and the gap between the water and quay was less than two feet. He tried to lift Mallon, to propel him towards the reaching hands, but he had no strength left. The cold consumed every part of him. Without the urge to keep Mallon safe, Roman might have given in to the impulse to close his eyes and slip away into the dark depths.

His arms were empty. The people above had gained purchase on his soaking charge and hauled him to safety. Then it was his turn. He tried to help but was a dead weight. Lifting his hand required too much effort.

Somehow, the people on the quay pulled him from the water, and he felt the hard pavement beneath his back. A coat was draped over him, and he heard concerned voices.

"Take it easy."

"An ambulance is on the way..."

He couldn't surrender to unconsciousness. He struggled into a sitting position. "Mallon. Mallon." *Where is he?*

"Your friend is okay, thanks to you," a kind voice told him.

"Is he breathing?" he asked weakly.

"He's alive. Don't worry for now."

He allowed the people around to comfort him. Another coat was draped around his shoulders, a hot drink brought to his lips.

"It's coffee. Sip it slowly," a woman said. "Nice and easy."

He wrapped his hands gratefully around the mug, still numb throughout.

Mallon was on the ground to his left. He was unconscious. Someone had brought a pile of tablecloths from one of the restaurants. They shook out one after another and draped them over his still body, trying to keep him warm. A man knelt beside him and rubbed him vigorously from chest to waist. They knew what they were doing.

Please be okay. Please hold on.

There were other voices, close by, raised in concern.

"Hey, you need to sit down. Help is on the way."

Roman turned to look.

Will, surrounded by four other people, struggled to his feet. He swayed, looking around, getting his bearings.

"Sit down," a woman pleaded with him. "You need medical help."

Will locked eyes with Roman. A wild, panicked expression flashed over his face. He pushed aside the concerned woman and staggered backwards. He was in better shape than either Roman or Mallon. He turned and set off along the quayside, slowly, staggering towards the city centre.

"Stop," Roman croaked.

"It's all right," someone told him. "Help will be here soon."

The people who had tried to help Will looked on in amazement as he lurched away from them, taking stuttering steps, limping on his injured leg.

"Stop him," Roman said. His voice had little volume. The people closest to Will couldn't hear him. He grabbed the wrist of a man close by. "Stop him," he urged. "He's the Blyham Strangler."

The man gawped. "What?"

"Don't let him get away," his voice grew louder as desperation returned. "He's the Strangler."

His words took an age to sink into the crowd.

"He's *what*?"

"The Strangler?"

Sensing the impending threat, Will quickened his pace, breaking into a half-run.

"He's getting away," Roman cried.

Finally, realisation dawned. Two young men and a woman grasped the meaning of what Roman had said.

"Stop the fucker," the woman yelled.

The three of them tore after him. Will moved even faster.

Roman watched as the three bystanders caught up with him. He lashed out with a fist, but cold, water-logged and injured, there was no strength behind the punch. The men grabbed him by each arm and spun him around.

As they marched him back towards the crowd, Roman heard sirens in the distance. The emergency services were on the way.

The nightmare was over.

Chapter Twenty-Four

"What happens now?"

Mallon was released from hospital on Saturday morning, following several days of treatment for hypothermia, shock, concussion and the knife wound to his chest. Roman, who had only suffered mild hypothermia, had been allowed home earlier in the week. The police had finished with the apartment when Roman was released, and he spent the time cleaning up and getting everything ready for Mallon's return. After all that had happened, he hadn't wanted to spend a night in the apartment alone and had gone back to his own place to sleep each night.

Mallon had spoken with his wife and had persuaded her not to come to England. He would visit her when he was well enough to fly, and they would make a decision about their future then. Roman had no idea what Mallon intended to do and was resolved not to influence him in any way. Mallon would have to make up his own mind.

The police had told them little about Will in the days since the incident. They assured them that he was being treated at a different hospital in another city and remained under constant guard. Roman had thought little of Will in the days that followed. The police had him in custody, and that was enough. His concerns lay with Mallon and how close they had come to losing each other.

On Saturday morning, Roman collected him from the hospital at ten-thirty. Mallon had changed a lot in a short space of time. The confidence and swagger Roman was used to had receded. He was less sure of himself and worried about Will and what would happen to him.

"I don't trust the laws in this country," he had told Roman during a visit on Thursday. "What if they let him go?"

"He's going nowhere but jail," Roman had assured him. Even if Will denied all the charges against him, the police had enough evidence to make sure he was remanded in custody until any trial. His chance of him getting away with any of his crimes appeared slim.

"You've lost weight," Roman said, as he wrapped an arm around Mallon's waist, walking him to the hospital entrance.

"Is it any surprise? The food in England is bad enough. What they serve in your hospitals is the worst."

Roman smiled. If Mallon was bitching about English food, it meant some of the old spunkiness was returning. "I'll find plenty to fatten you up when you get home."

Mallon hugged him tighter. "The only thing I need is you."

Roman had visited Mallon's favourite bakery when it had opened that morning and when they reached the apartment, it smelled of fresh pastries and coffee. Roman had set a pot of his favourite on to brew before leaving for the hospital.

"I wasn't sure how I would feel returning," Mallon said.

Roman helped him out his coat and guided him to the sofa. "This is your place. He was only here for an hour at most. He hasn't left an imprint."

Mallon stared at the sliding doors, unconvinced. "We'll have to keep those fucking things locked – or move up to a higher floor."

Roman set a plate of baked goodies on the table and poured two steaming cups of coffee. "See how you feel in a couple of weeks. It might not be as bad as you think." He flopped beside Mallon on the sofa and held him close. "He can't do anything to hurt us now."

Around midday they received a visitor. Roman was surprised to open the door and find DS Benito Coppola standing there. He'd seen the detective from a distance several times that week, around the hospital and the apartment as the police investigation into Will developed at pace.

"Hi," Benito said. "I hope you don't mind me stopping by. I went to the hospital, but they told me the two of you had left already."

"Is this an official call?" Roman asked. Despite their good work this week, his hostility towards the police had not decreased. The Blyham Strangler had not been apprehended and stopped because of any ingenuity or investigation on their part. He'd been captured by chance and his own carelessness. If he hadn't come for Mallon, he would still be at large, free to kill again and again.

"It is," Benito said. "I have news."

Roman opened the door and stood aside. "You'd better come in." He led Benito to the living room and ignoring the good manners he'd been raised with — didn't offer him a drink or one of the delicious pastries. He sat beside Mallon and held his hand. "Well?"

Benito took a seat across from them. "Last night, we charged Will Hadley, whose real name is actually Lewis Braemer, with seven counts of murder."

Mallon's sharp intake of breath hissed through his teeth.

"Together with the two counts of attempted murder against yourselves... He appeared at Blyham magistrates court this morning and has been remanded for an appearance at crown court next week. We expect him to plead not guilty, though there is no chance of him going anywhere. He'll be held in custody until a trial can take place."

"Then he is the Strangler? There's no doubt about that?

"Absolutely. It's him."

"How?" Roman asked. "Just because he attacked us, what makes you sure he killed all those other men?"

Benito bit his lip and gazed at his hands, seeming to consider his answer. "This is off the record. It can't go any further. I'm only telling you this to allay any fears you might have that the killer is still out there. I could get fired if this comes out." He took a deep breath. "But fuck it. We found photos of all the victims on his phone. Post-mortem images. There's no doubt that it's him."

"Shit." Nausea brimmed in Roman's stomach. *I slept with him. I went to bed with a killer. That fucking piece of shit.*

"As I said, Will Hadley is an alias," Benito continued. "One of many, but it seems to be the one he favoured whenever he was here. Lewis Braemar lives in Birmingham. He's married, has no children and is a rep for a pharmaceutical company. His work takes him all over the Northeast and Northwest."

"Fuck."

"What I have just told you cannot leave this room. Understand?"

Roman had already made the connection. "You think he's done it elsewhere, don't you? There could be other victims, all over the fucking country."

Benito nodded grimly. "Which is why you can't tell anyone. I've already said too much. If this gets out, it could jeopardise other investigations."

"We understand," Mallon said, putting a hand on top of Roman's, squeezing.

"But why us?" Roman asked. "What made us his target? And only days after Phil."

"We don't know. We're still putting together a picture of his methods. But from what we can ascertain, he chose his victims in advance, sometimes months ahead. He seduced them and gained their trust. Then later, he broke into their homes and killed them.

"The truth is I planned to kill you last October." Roman remembered the words Will had said in this very room a few nights ago. He'd been biding his time, waiting for the right moment. He blinked back tears as the full horror dawned on him. "How did he get in? How did he go undetected?"

"We don't have all the answers. He's ex-army, served five years before leaving the service. You witnessed yourself how physically fit he is...and cunning. If we keep digging, we're sure to unearth some burglaries in his past. I think he's been getting away with this kind of thing for much longer than we know about."

* * * *

"It's me," Roman said. "I'm the reason he came after you."

They were in bed later that afternoon. The curtains were closed against the low winter sun. They lay side by side beneath the covers, staring at the ceiling. They had recently had sex. It had been an act of urgency and defiance, two men taking comfort from each other's bodies and the fact that they were both alive.

"He came after me because he was fucked," Mallon said, tapping his forehead. "In here. You can't blame yourself what he did."

"You heard what Benito said. He chose his victims in advance and slept with them. I had sex with him last year, weeks before I met you. He must have planned to kill me way back then."

"But he didn't," Mallon said softy. "You're here with me, and he's in prison. And he's going to rot in there for the rest of his life, unless someone ends it for him first."

Roman struggled to remember much of his time with Will. They had met at The Viaduct and had gone back to Roman's flat. "I don't even remember much about the night he picked me up."

"What does it matter now?"

"It matters. I'll have to give evidence at his trial, and I need to be clear about the facts. I can't give his defence a single reason to shred my version of events."

Mallon rolled onto his side, moving carefully. The injury to his chest still caused him a lot of discomfort.

Mallon slid his hand across Roman's torso and rested it on his rib cage, right above his heart. "He's a liar and a killer. The police have enough to put him away already. What you remember about a one-night last year won't make much difference. They'll nail the bastard."

"I hope you're right." The idea that Mallon could be dead because of a madman's obsession with Roman sickened him. Beneath the covers, he linked his fingers with Mallon's upon his chest. "I came so close to losing you."

Mallon squeezed him back. "I almost lost you, too," he said, his voice barely above a whisper. "But I didn't."

Gently Roman rolled onto his side to face him. His drew his fingertips along the side of Mallon's face before leaning in to kiss him on the mouth, and the jaw, then he carefully eased Mallon onto his back and climbed on top of him. Mallon snaked his hands around his waist, and Roman felt the sudden hardness of his cock. He reached between his legs to guide him into position then lowered himself, taking him inside.

He moved slowly, barely at all to begin with, not wanting to put a strain on Mallon's injuries. Roman leaned forward, pressing his body against him, while bearing the weight. Mallon ground upwards, burying his cock deeper until they were overcome with urgency once more. They thrust against each other until Mallon released a gentle growl, his brow furrowing. Roman stroked his own cock and timed his swelling climax close to perfection.

The afternoon grew dark outside. Mallon turned on the sidelights, but they remained in bed, curled on their sides and facing each other once more.

"What happens now?" Roman asked at last. "Before Will attacked you, we were facing a different kind of problem."

Mallon's pale eyes glistened in the low light. "Coming close to death puts other issues in perspective." He shuffled closer. "I love you," he said breathlessly.

Tears welled and spilled down Roman's face. "I love you, too."

"I'm getting a divorce."

Relief flooded through him. "You are?"

"I've already discussed it with Betrice."

"When?"

"Thursday night. She called. We agreed that we have stayed together for the wrong reasons. We can't waste the next eight or nine years of our lives when I have the chance to be happy right now."

"Do you mean that?"

"Every word. I will have to go back to France to make arrangements with Betrice and our lawyers. And I need to see my children. But I want to start a new life here...with you."

Roman moved closer and wrapped his arms around him. This was real, not a dream. He was in Mallon's bed, holding him, and he had just said the words Roman had been desperate to hear. They had almost lost their lives a few nights before, and now they had a brand-new future together.

He had learned how fragile life could be and how quickly it could be over. Roman intended to grasp every opportunity that came his way, and there was none greater than the man in his arms right then.

Sign up for our newsletter and find out about all our romance book releases, eBook sales and promotions, sneak peeks and FREE romance books!

Want to see more from this author?
Here's a taster for you to enjoy!

Basic Instincts:
Nothing But the Night
Thom Collins

Excerpt

The luxury of a good night's sleep was something Marc Glass had learnt to live without. For several years he'd been getting by on three to four hours. Five was a rare indulgence. He couldn't bear to lie in bed, idly staring into the dark, knowing there was no chance of falling off again. As soon as his eyes opened, he was wide awake. Two years earlier he had taken up late-night running, in the hope that physical exhaustion would be the trigger he needed for a full night of rest. While it helped him to fall asleep quickly, he still found himself alert at four a.m. most mornings.

Usually, he would get straight up and begin work, but some days, like this one, he pulled on his running shoes and went for another pre-dawn run.

It had gone six-thirty as he pounded the coastal path on the return route to the house. He had been out for an hour. The darkness and cold of a wet March morning did not deter him. He didn't feel the cold or the drizzle when he was running. A podcast on Blyham history in the eighteenth century had occupied his mind for most of the course. Now that it had finished, his mind turned to the day ahead.

There was a sliver of light grey sky on the horizon. Sunrise was about half an hour away. The forecast was for cloud and rain for the rest of the week. Typical Blyham weather for this time of year. Not that it mattered. Marc had a full day of meetings planned, both at the factory and online with overseas buyers. There was a good chance he wouldn't breathe fresh air again until his night-time run that evening, and he was already looking forward to the next episode of the podcast.

Through the week, one day was much like another. A cycle of exercise and work peppered with a couple of visits to his parents. They would cook dinner for him one evening and he would take then out for a meal on the other. Tonight, he had to fend for himself. He'd stay late at the factory to delay his return to an empty house. Probably pick up some food on his way home. Nothing too heavy. Not when he'd have to run it off later.

The drizzle strengthened into rain. Marc swiped his arm across his face, wiping the sweat and water away.

He still had his ear-pods in, but could hear the violent crash of waves below, battering the rocky outcrop beneath the cliffs. It sounded like things were getting rougher than had been forecast. If a storm was coming in, he'd just have to complete his evening exercises in his home gym, though he preferred the freshness and exposure of a night run.

Almost home, he put on an extra burst of speed for the last mile, coming off the track and onto the main road that led to the house. His breath rasped, searing his lungs and throat, pain burning in his thighs and calf muscles, but he powered through. Pain was good. Pain was a real sensation. It meant he was still alive.

As he turned onto the drive he saw a strange car parked in front of the garage. A dark BMW.

Marc slowed to a stop. His breath grated in his ears, and he removed the pods. He sucked in a chest full of air through his mouth. His heart pounded.

The driver's door of the car opened, and an umbrella poked out and was put up. A woman with blonde hair stepped from the car. She was petite, in a pale trouser suit and impractical high heels. Marc rubbed his eyes and blinked away the stinging sweat, trying to focus. There was something familiar about the woman.

She approached with a tight, humourless smile. Beneath the umbrella, her hair was a blow-dried miracle. She must have got up as early as he had to achieve that look.

"I'd heard you were an early riser," she said. Elocution and speech training couldn't mask the original Geordie tones in her accent. "I thought I had already missed you. Ten more minutes and I was going to head over to the factory."

Marc froze as he realised just who his visitor was.

Nadine Smythe.

He stepped around her, heading for the house. "You wasted your time coming here."

The rain turned into a downpour. He took shelter beneath the front porch. He left the key under a rock in the garden when he went running, but he didn't want to retrieve it in front of Nadine. She would think nothing of letting herself in another time.

"I've come about your brother," she said, stepping onto the porch. She put down the umbrella and shook it out. "Awful morning, isn't it? I should have brought a raincoat but it was dry when I left home."

"You shouldn't be here at all. I've got nothing to say to you."

"Don't be like that. You should be pleased someone cares enough about Theo to follow up the story."

"My brother is not a story," he snapped.

Nadine Smythe was a journalist for *The Blyham Chronicle*. She also had her own podcast where she *"exposed injustices and laid bare the truth."* She was beginning to gain fame beyond local news and had appeared on several national breakfast and mid-morning TV shows offering her opinions on news and current events. Her opinions were always bombastically right wing.

"You're wrong there," she said, her cold stare boring into him. "I've been working on this for several weeks and there's most definitely a story. And I'm going to tell it. I'm giving you the opportunity to be part of it. To put your family's position across."

"I think you've done enough damage to me and my family already. The answer is no. Now get back in your car and take it off my drive."

"I think Theo was murdered." She let the words drop like bombs, studying his face for a reaction.

Marc had learnt the hard way to keep his emotions to himself. He would never allow a hack like Nadine to read him.

His face was stone.

Inside he was a mess.

She had given voice to the words he had only dared to think.

"He's been dead three months," he managed to say. "Why your sudden interest?"

Nadine edged closer. "There's nothing sudden about it. I was researching a story that involved Theo before he died. When his death appeared to be an accident, I thought I had lost my lead. I was wrong."

"What are talking about?" Marc made no effort to hide the contempt in his voice. As well as stoking the rage of the Alt-right, Nadine's podcast was big on conspiracy theories. He doubted she believed most of the shit she shared, but she wouldn't let something as trivial as her personal beliefs get in the way of her rising profile.

"Your brother was involved with some important people. You know that much, right? He was a sex worker. A popular one, by all accounts."

And there it was. The true reason for her interest. A salacious sex scandal. A *gay* sex scandal at that. He could already hear the indignant tone of her broadcast. The moral outrage her reports would stir up. "Leave," he snapped, jabbing his finger towards the road.

"Theo was killed because of what he knew. Because of *whom* he knew. I know you don't like me, Marc, but you must care about seeing justice done. For the sake of your little brother. C'mon, surely you can put our differences aside to get to the truth."

"Theo was killed in a hit-and-run. It was an accident."

"And the driver has never been traced. The car was stolen and burnt without a scrap of evidence remaining. I don't believe you're satisfied with that conclusion. Not when your brother was providing sexual services to a Tory back-bencher."

He raised his hand. "Enough…" Anxiety wrapped its suffocating tendrils around his chest. His breath was fast and shallow. He closed his eyes and fought against it, disgusted with himself for allowing her to see that she had got to him.

"I'm not looking to trash Theo's memory. I promise that. Theo was a small part of a bigger story. An important part. I believe he lost his life because of it. We can put that right and expose the people behind it."

Theo Glass had been no saint. Marc was aware of that. He didn't know the details of everything his brother had been involved in, but he knew enough. Theo had taken delight in shocking him, bragging about his online content. About how many followers he had on social media, how many paid subscribers there were for his sexual site. Marc had seen how far Theo went with the images and videos he posted on his open X profile. He didn't want to know what he was doing behind the paywall of Hot-4-Fans and other subscription sites. There was escorting too. Like a lot of younger people, Theo believed he was from the first generation to embrace sex and pleasure. He thought he could provoke his older brother with the details of his life. Theo hadn't realised that Marc wasn't shocked. The truth was he just wasn't interested. He had bigger problems than worrying about his brother selling his arse to wealthy older men. All that mattered was that Theo didn't tell their parents what he was doing.

If Nadine went ahead with this muck-raking article, there would no way of keeping it from them. They had a copy of *The Blyham Chronicle* delivered each morning. Their hearts hadn't recovered from the death of their youngest son. The shock of how he'd earnt a living might finish them off.

"Please, Nadine, don't do this. The police are still investigating his death. Leave it to them."

"Blyham police," she sneered. "They don't give a shit. The case remains open in name only. There's not a single officer actively investigating. C'mon, wake up. Your brother was fucking the Member of Parliament for Blyham South. The pressure from above to make this disappear is immense."

"You know that for a fact?"

"Of course I fucking do. I've got contacts in the force who have told me exactly that."

"On the record?"

She rolled her eyes. "What do you think? They want to keep their jobs."

"Then you've got nothing. This is more of your conspiracy bullshit. It plays well on those crappy news channels you go on, but it's not reality. Now go, before I call the police to move you on. And if you doorstep me like this again, I'll phone your editor and report you for harassment."

Nadine accepted defeat and put up her umbrella. "This isn't harassment, it's journalism. Whether you like it or not, your brother's death is part of a story and I'm going to write it. If you want to do justice to his memory, you know where to find me."

Marc stood on the porch and watched her walk back to the car. He waited until she was inside and had started the engine. The rain bounced six inches off the roof as she reversed into a U-turn and drove away. The sky had lightened to a miserable shade of grey.

Fuck.

He'd known when he'd woken up at four this morning that this was going to be a shitty day and his instinct had been correct.

Marc retrieved the hidden key and went into the house. He kicked off his muddy running shoes at the front door and strode to the kitchen in his socks. His mind galloped ahead, so much information rushing through his brain. He'd had dealings with Nadine Smythe before. She was dangerous, borderline psychopathic in his opinion, but she was determined. She thought she was on to a big story and that was it. She wouldn't let it go. The sensational detail of his brother's life prior to his death would be exposed and scandalised in her shitty newspaper and podcast. He could already see her sitting on a breakfast TV sofa, smug in her moral superiority, delighting in the shock she caused, oblivious to the devastation her story would bring.

Marc couldn't allow it. His parents had suffered enough. Theo had died in early December. Marc had thought their first Christmas without him was going to break them, but they'd got through it. Their grief was tottering on the edge of the acceptance stage.

Nadine Smythe would set them right back.

Unless he did something about it.

About the Author

Thom Collins is the author of Closer by Morning, with Pride Publishing. His love of page turning thrillers began at an early age when his mother caught him reading the latest Jackie Collins book and promptly confiscated it, sparking a life-long love of raunchy novels.

Thom has lived in the North East of England his whole life. He grew up in Northumberland and now lives in County Durham with his husband and two cats. He loves all kinds of genre fiction, especially bonkbusters, thrillers, romance and horror. He is also a cookery book addict with far too many titles cluttering his shelves. When not writing he can be found in the kitchen trying out new recipes. He's a keen traveler but with a fear of flying that gets worse with age, but since taking his first cruise in 2013 he realized that sailing is the way to go.

Thom loves to hear from readers. You can find his contact information, website details and author profile page at https://www.firstforromance.com

ENTWINED PUBLISHING

Meet Amber Kell

Amber Kell has made a career out of daydreaming. It has been a lifelong habit she practices diligently as shown by her complete lack of focus on anything not related to her fantasy world building.

When she told her husband what she wanted to do with her life, he told her to go have fun.

During those seconds she isn't writing, she remembers she has children who humor her with games of 'what if' and let her drag them to foreign lands to gather inspiration. Her youngest confided in her that he wants to write because he longs for a website and an author name—two things apparently necessary to be a proper writer.

Despite her husband's insistence she doesn't drink enough to be a true literary genius, she continues to spin stories of people falling happily in love and staying that way.

She is thwarted during the day by a traffic jam of cats on the stairway and a puppy who insists on walks, but she bravely perseveres.

amberkell.wordpress.com
amberkellwrites@gmail.com